Books by Shirley Rousseau Murphy

The Grass Tower
Silver Woven in My Hair

SILVER WOVEN
IN MY HAIR

SILVER WOVEN IN MY HAIR

by Shirley Rousseau Murphy

ILLUSTRATED BY

Alan Tiegreen

ATHENEUM · New York · 1977

For Megan Kiley
A very special niece

The Cinderella stories came, in large part, from
Cinderella: Three Hundred and Forty-five Variants . . .
by Marian Roalfe Cox. Published for the Folk-Lore Society
by David Nutt, London, 1893.

Library of Congress Cataloging in Publication Data

Murphy, Shirley Rousseau.   Silver woven in my hair.

[1. Civilization, Medieval—Fiction]   I. Tiegreen,
Alan.   II. Title.
PZ7.M956Si   [Fic]   76-25578
ISBN 978-1-4814-5865-8

Published simultaneously in Canada by
McClelland & Stewart, Ltd.
Manufactured in the United States of America by
The Book Press
Brattleboro, Vermont
Designed by Mary M. Ahern
First Edition

SILVER WOVEN
IN MY HAIR

Crystal shoes
And a mare to ride on,
A milk white mare,
And silver woven in my hair.

Chapter One

THE night wind blew down from the rocky hills and swept the cobbled streets clean. It brushed the dust of the high road as smooth as velvet, as if no dogcart or carriage had ever traveled it; but now in the gray dawn the velvet dust was freshly marked with hoofprints. Wandering, aimless hoofprints that began at the inn behind the village and ended at the edge of the cobbles.

Following the hoofprints came a barefoot girl, her eyes still heavy with sleep. She might have been sixteen, but her hair was down like a child's, and her childish dress far too small—as if someone did not allow her to put on the airs of a grown woman. Her wrists and ankles protruded, and were goose-pimply in the cold.

She had ragtaggle hair the color of new hay, and

3

her eyes were the blue of batchelor buttons. (Her step-sister Druscilla said blue eyes were ugly as dung.) She had a tip-tilted nose (Delilah scoffed at such a nose) and the curves beneath her dress were supple and fine. (Though the two stepsisters called her a baby, scrawny as a new-hatched chicken.) Her skimpy dress was faded and mended; and her feet were streaked with cinders from the hearth, for she had been stirring up the fire when she glanced out the kitchen window, saw the gate open, and knew the mare was gone.

The sun had not yet risen, nor the village stirred. Two geese hunkered after snails, and a chicken scratched in the cobbled gutter.

Thursey paused in the center of the village, shivered once with the chill, and felt the smooth cobbles with her toes. The predawn stillness quite pleased her.

It was a small, shabby village. The tinker's shop was cramped, the smithy's roof was badly in need of thatching, and the weaver's shop was no more than a drafty lean-to that sheltered the elbowing loom. Even the church was small and wanted paint. A drake sat atop the brewer's shutter, eyeing a row of ale kegs that stood outside the door.

The cobbles felt smooth and hard; she curled her toes around them as she walked and stared into the dark alleys that ran between the shops. It would do no good to call the mare, wilful old thing! It seemed to Thursey that half her life was spent searching for the mare (the other half was spent scrubbing the hearth, cleaning the stable, cooking the meals for travelers— though she didn't begrudge *that*—and cleaning up the kitchen afterward), and she wondered why the old mare was always so tricky and obstinate. But I suppose, Thursey thought, if she always minded me I would not love her at all, for then she wouldn't be herself, now would she? The sun was beginning to send a bit of rosy glimmer over the hills when she spied the old mare's rump blocking the far end of the alley between the weaver's and the bakery shop; the mare was leaning over the weaver's fence stealing hay from the sheep. The sheep began to bleat up a terrible fuss, standing on their hind legs against the fence. The mare's wide rump filled the alley, and she had her tail tucked down stubbornly. At the other end of her, her ears were tight back, for she had seen Thursey—the old hoyden saw as well behind as in front—and was set to resist the pulls and coaxings she knew were coming.

The alley was so narrow Thursey had to squeeze flat and hold her breath to get between the wall and the mare's fat side. The culvert in the alley stank of night soil where the chamber pots had been dumped, and the bakery smelled of dough rising in the cool dark.

The mare smelled of sweat. The marks of yesterday's harness were still on her dirty white sides, for Thursey had not had time to wash her. Thursey slipped a bit of rope around the mare's neck, then leaned against the bony chest and pushed until the graceless animal began to back out reluctantly, showing her long yellow teeth in anger.

When they were free of the alley, Thursey hoisted her skirts and tucked them round, pulled herself up by the mare's mane, threw a leg over, and was astride. The mare shook her head menacingly and Thursey laughed at her. (If Druscilla and Delilah could see her, they would shriek with horror; girls and women did not ride astride and certainly did not show their legs!) Thursey grinned and kicked the old mare in the ribs, pushing her forward into a canter to avoid the jerky trot.

The mare lolloped clumsily down the cobbles and onto the soft lane. Then, not wanting to go home, she drew to a walk and Thursey let her, for the morning was sweet with the smell of wet grass and turned earth. A cold freshness came from the hills, and the smell of watercress and mint blew up to them from the little stream. They went down to it and Thursey let the mare

dredge up mouthfuls of watercress; it would give her hiccups, but she loved it so.

Thursey slipped off the mare and pulled her dress over her head. (If Druscilla and Delilah saw *that*, they would faint dead away. Her stepmother, Augusta, would beat her and call her a harlot.) She jumped into the cold stream, and the icy water shocked her to her toes. She bathed until she tingled, then she dressed and lay in the dewy grass and thought about the traveler who was staying at the inn overnight, and about the tale he had told. He was a fat little man, a merchant, and the story he told was wonderful, of a maid called Aschenputtel. Thursey, with no one to hear, began to make a song about it. She sang it to the mare, though the old white head never stopped pushing after watercress, and the mare's jaws never stopped chewing.

> *"Hazel tree, O see my plight,*
> *Hazel tree, O will you bring,*
> *Golden dress and crystal shoes,*
> *A mare to ride on, a milk white mare,*
> *And silver woven in my hair . . ."*

Suddenly she remembered the porridge. She leaped up in alarm, scrambled onto the mare's back, and kicked her so hard the mare lolloped for home like the devil was after her.

The kitchen smelled of burning. Druscilla was fanning an apron at the smoke and swearing loudly. Delilah waved the scorched kettle helplessly. "Where have you been, you lazy baggage, look what a mess you've made!"

"The whole place smells of burning," screamed Druscilla.

Thursey said nothing. She began a second kettle of porridge and laid slabs of bacon on the grate. The stepsisters flounced out, bearing the bread and hot ale. "When you've dished up a proper breakfast," Druscilla flung over her shoulder, "see to the gentleman's horse!"

Thursey made a face at the door and whispered, "Fish eye!"

It was true, Druscilla had eyes like the eyes of a fish that had been fried with its head on: bulging. The name Druscilla meant soft-eyed, and Druscilla never forgot it. She believed herself to be beautiful and would stare at a young man (or any man) with what she thought was a warm and seductive gaze until he grew so uneasy, he would fidget and turn away from her. Then she would say to Delilah, "He's so *shy* of me, he cannot bear my beauty."

Thursey heated more ale and stirred the porridge.

Delilah's name meant temptress, and Thursey

9

thought, She couldn't tempt a billy goat in rut. But Delilah, fat as a young stoat, wore the dresses of a temptress anyway, and if the men stared at such a quantity of bare skin it was only out of shock—or to avoid having to look higher, at Delilah's face. (Her face resembled a pig, certainly it did.) Where Delilah's face was fat, Druscilla's was as thin as a saw blade and just as fearsome, with the two fishy eyes staring out. And both had sat simpering at the traveler last night in the hall until Thursey, who was watching from the shadows, thought he might run screaming into the night. Poor little man, pudgy and bearded and harmless looking. Those two would go after anything that wore trousers, she thought indignantly. But there was another reason the stepsisters were so friendly to him. He had arrived in a fine carriage laden with wonders to trade, embroidered purses from Italy and jewelry from Spain, silver ladles and pewter trays, bracelets and pearl-encrusted girdles and ribbons of all the colors one could imagine. He carried cotton from Egypt and cloth of silk from Venice, dainties to intrigue any woman; he carried spices and scents and ermine tails, and the sisters, beside themselves with greed, nearly came to blows over him.

Thursey smiled. The merchant had paid little heed

to the stepsisters; and he had given them no gift. The only gift he made was the one he gave to Thursey and didn't know he gave. For as she had crouched in the shadows of the hall after supper and watched her stepmother, Augusta, and the two stepsisters simper and preen, the merchant had begun his story. And Thursey, curled in her dark corner, had listened with pleasure.

Thursey was not encouraged in the hall: the sisters said she was too common, that she would afront the travelers. But when a traveler looked as if he might sing a ballad or tell a tale, she would slip into the shadows after the platters were washed up, settle herself beside a friendly spider web, warm in the rushes, and wait.

The inn was small and had seen better days, but it was the only inn for a day's ride that would offer bed to the commoners on the high road. This wealthy merchant would have been welcome at the palace that gleamed atop the rocky hills to the west, but the king's entourage had not yet arrived from the southern villa where the king spent his winters, and the palace was closed and unwelcoming. When the king's party did come, it would come upon the high road in a bustling caravan. Everyone who traveled across the small country of Gies used the high road, from king's messengers to peddlers, from friars to jugglers to gleemen; and the robbers who preyed on them traveled in the shadow of the woods.

Travelers came to the village from all over Gies itself, and beyond, and they were the only source of news. They brought messages and gossip, ballads of wars, and best of all the stories. From Wales and Ireland and France and from countries so small one had never heard of them, came stories of the kind Thursey loved best. Tales of girls who, their feet grimed from the hearth, were banished to the kitchen and stables and treated cruelly by their elders. Each story was different from the next, each told with the flavor of its own country's ways. But in each there was a girl Thursey could not help but weep for, Cendrillon or Rushencoatie, Vasilisa or Hajnalka or Cari Woodencoat. She wept for Cinderella and for the Snow White Maid, for Tattercoats and Cap-O-Rushes, for the King's Daughter in the Mound, and now she wept for Aschenputtel. She had crouched in the rushes and listened to the tale, and she might have been twelve again and her father telling her stories before the fire at night.

The stepsisters would scoff and call her childish to be occupied with such frippery—they listened not with interest, but for a night's entertainment. It could have been a list of supplies and accounts as long as it was a man's voice ringing through the hall. But the stories freed Thursey from her stepmother and stepsisters in a manner she could not explain; it hurt no one, the strength she took from them.

She turned the bacon and put some bread on the grate to toast; the fireplace was so big she stood inside when she moved the kettles, her cheeks flushed from the heat. Red cheeks made Druscilla and Delilah cross with envy; and Thursey took a perverse pleasure in that.

The kitchen was a plain room, with hewn timbers, a floor of rushes, and a plank for a table. Thursey kept the table scrubbed; the jars and ale jugs and crocks and platters shone from her care. The kitchen was the best room in the inn, though Delilah and Druscilla called it ugly. They thought the stable ugly, too; they never went there, except to the mounting block where they would step into their high black carriage behind Magniloquence, their bad-tempered black mare. Off they would go, the two overdressed sisters and the black robed, sour stepmother, to mass of a Sunday. The stepmother, Augusta, was as lumpish and square as a dung cart, great boxlike creature dressed in rusty black dresses that smelled of mildew and were stained with the drippings of ale and gravy—she loved her ale, Augusta, but would let the sisters have none. She said it would spoil their complexions. As for Thursey, ale was too good for the likes of her. Off to mass the three would go, behind the mettlesome Magniloquence, while Thursey stayed at home with the old white mare for company.

There had been a time in the stepmother's younger days when she had ridden out in some style on the sidesaddle that now gathered dust in the harness room. That had been when Thursey's father was alive, and Augusta was not so haughty and set in her ungiving ways.

Occasionally even now in a strange fit of nostalgia, Augusta would bid Thursey bring the sidesaddle and bridle and polish them, and put them on the black mare —though Magniloquence would throw a tantrum until they were removed again.

And the white mare, of course, was considered far too common to carry such a saddle, certainly too common to carry Augusta. Poor ugly mare. She had great oversized joints, her knees and hocks were swollen and lumpy, and her ragged, splayed hooves were never shod. Her dirty white coat was so sprinkled with black hairs that she looked as if she'd been rolling in the pepper, and now, in the early spring, she was shedding her winter coat in ragged hanks so she looked altogether moth-eaten. "Tattercoats," Thursey whispered. "You are Tattercoats." But it was only an endearment, the old mare had no name. Thursey preferred it that way. If she called her by a name, the sisters would take note of it, take note of the mare, and discover that Thursey loved her.

The mare had loppy ears, one with a notch out as if someone had taken a bite from it (as indeed an ardent stallion had when she was a young filly), and she was kept only to haul fodder and dung. There were stalls in the stables for Magniloquence, and for the travelers' horses and donkeys, for it took a poor man, indeed, to travel the high road without some kind of mount. But the old mare was not allowed a stall; she slept in the stable yard winter and summer and got only the leavings of hay (or so she was supposed to do; Thursey saw that she got better than that).

It was to the old mare that Thursey went when she was lonely or hurt, or smarting from the insults Delilah and Druscilla gave or the tongue-lashings Augusta was so skilled at. Thursey could dream away the mare's misshapen legs and boney Roman nose, could dream her into a milk-white steed as delicate and fine as any

15

lady's palfrey that came down the high road. A pristine mount with skin as pink as the magical roses that were said to grow in the swamp and legs as thin and smooth as Thursey's own ankles. And a silver saddle hung with white satin, and Thursey in a frock of scarlet like the cloth she had seen in the merchant's cart, and her hair braided in a great coil, with strands of silver woven in. Beside her would ride a prince, young and comely; she would be truly a woman grown, and beautiful.

She brought herself back from daydreaming with a quick shake of her head and rescued the bacon from burning. When she had served the meal, she went to the stable yard and fed and watered the fussing Magniloquence and the merchant's sturdy bay gelding. Then she curried them both, the gelding standing patiently and wrinkling his skin with pleasure at the feel of the brush, blowing his warm breath on her neck, then Magniloquence, as fidgety and bad tempered as if she had a bee under her tail. She would have swung around and kicked Thursey if Thursey had not kept her tied short. When both horses were groomed, Thursey took up the currycomb and combed out her own tangled hair, peering at her reflection in the water trough. The sun glanced off the fresh straw around her feet and made it shine like silver. She picked up a strand and when she turned it a certain way it did, indeed, look like silver. She held it to her hair and gazed down at her reflection. The straw sparkled up at her. The darkness of the water made her face look older, look almost mysterious. Deftly she wove the straw into her hair, wove another and another until a net of silver shone around her face.

"Imbecile!" a voice shouted. Thursey froze, then looked up to see Delilah, her broad shadow cast across the water trough. "Can't you even come out to curry the horses without playing like a child! You look like you fell in the hay. Get that mess out of your hair."

Thursey began to pull out the straws.

"Why you've put them in on purpose!" Delilah peered closer. "You put them in on purpose," she repeated and began to laugh. She guffawed, roared with laughter, slapped her side and brayed. "You've woven your hair with straw—*with straw!* What'd you think it was, precious stones and gold?"

Thursey blanched, then turned red.

Delilah stared at her. "Oh, wait 'til I tell Ma! Oh, oh," and she fell into further paroxysms of laughter. She could have been heard clear to the castle if there had been anyone there to hear her.

Thursey glared. The sisters had never dared act so

17

cruel before her father went away. He would have set Delilah straight. But now if she mentioned him, Delilah would only scoff and say, "That coward! Your father died a coward running from the Balkskakian hordes." She'd heard that more times than she could count. *Would* her father come home one day? Things hadn't been right since he left. She turned away from Delilah now with angry tears.

I could go away, she thought. But if I did, and he is alive, he wouldn't find me here. And the inn is rightfully his; it's not their inn at all.

"I should turn the likes of you out," Augusta would threaten often. But that wasn't likely. Who would scrub and cook and mind the stable? No one, not for free anyway. "Your father's dead. We could turn you out."

I don't know that he's dead, Thursey thought. No one knows what happened to him in the battles with Balkskak.

Chapter Two

THURSEY'S bed was a cupboard in the kitchen wall. Under it were shelves where the pots and pans were kept, and flanking it were the great fireplace on one side and the broom closet on the other. The bed itself had doors that could be shut and locked, though it had been a long time since Augusta had locked Thursey into it—when she was a good deal smaller. At the back of the cupboard were narrow shelves for Thursey's other dress, her night dress, and her few meager possessions.

Late at night, with the noises of the inn stilled and the sisters upstairs in their beds, with the hoot of an owl coming through the open window and the smoldering fire throwing shadows on the walls, Thursey could imagine any exciting thing. This night the moon was full, sending its light into the kitchen. Thursey drew

her quilt around her and watched moonlight and fire-
light mingle to cast strange shapes across the room,
as if a shadowy play were being enacted there. She
thought of the story the merchant had told, and how the
dear father had said, "What shall I bring you from
the fair?" One stepdaughter had replied, "Bring me a
cloak of pearls and jewels and bring me a fan of silver,"
and the other had cried, "Bring me a mirror that I can
see my beauty; bring me an emerald comb for my raven
hair." Thursey watched the light play across the black
stewpot and skillets, and they seemed to be figures
moving. "And what will I bring you?" The father asked
Aschenputtel. "Bring me, O Father, the first twig that
strikes your hat as you leave the fair."

Thursey wriggled her cold feet and pictured Aschenputtel planting the hazel twig her father brought her,
placing it in the earth upon her mother's grave. Each
day Aschenputtel wept upon it, and soon the twig
sprouted leaves and grew into a hazel tree. Each day
that Aschenputtel wept over it, it grew larger. And
each time she prayed over it, a white bird came to sit on
a branch and speak to her.

When Aschenputtel was forbidden by her stepmother to go to the king's festival, the white bird said,
"You must go." Aschenputtel replied, "But I have no

dress to wear." And the bird said, "Do as I say, and you shall have." Thursey pictured Aschenputtel kneeling before the hazel tree and repeating the words as the bird instructed, "Little tree, little tree, shake over me, that silver and gold may come down and cover me." And at once she was wearing a dress of silver and slippers made of gold. And the next night the dress and slippers were finer, and the night after, finer still; and the mounts that stood before her of a beauty beyond belief. Thursey could see it plainly. She lit a candle and reached under her straw mattress.

She pulled away a bit of wood and drew from the hole a bit of sacking. From this she took paints and precious paper. Then she closed the cupboard doors, wishing she could latch them from inside.

She painted long into the night, page after page that would become a book telling Aschenputtel's tale. She made the pictures around the edges of each page and wrote the story in the middle. She painted the two ugly sisters, the twig, the tree, the white bird, the gold and silver dresses.

It had been an old monk passing on the high road who had taught her to write and to paint. A monk dressed in a dusty brown habit and riding a donkey so small Thursey wondered it could carry the rotund

21

old man, an old monk with paper and colors and quills. He had stayed at the inn healing from an ailment, paying for his board with prayers (which the sisters had little use for) and handiwork (which they used in plenty). He took Thursey into the wood and taught her the herbs to pick so she could have color: saffron and blueberry and madder, indigo and sumac and oak. He gave her paper and made her a brush from the soft hair that she pulled from the old mare's currycomb. Then he taught her letters, a secret she must surely keep to herself, for in those days few could read, and those of a low caste who could do so might be suspected of enchantments.

They had done it all on the sly, the monk saying that he begged Thursey's help in gathering herbs for his fever, and for his good works. The sisters, afraid of some higher wrath if they refused, gave her over reluctantly. Augusta had scowled, remarking that her duties were in the kitchen, not the fields. Anwin had paid them no attention. "Keep your secrets, child. Those three biddies would have your head if they didn't need you in the kitchen. Someday, you'll see, a great enchantment will come to you just as in the stories. Don't laugh, it will surely happen." He had winked at Thursey and at the old mare. The mare had snorted

23

back at him, and Thursey had grinned at them both.

She drew a border of hazel leaves for the cover of "Aschenputtel" and painted the white bird in the center. Tomorrow she would sew the pages together.

The books satisfied something in Thursey, and she guarded her secret fiercely; though once, late at night, Druscilla had slipped in unheard and seen the candle-light beneath the closed doors of Thursey's bed. Thursey, hearing a rustle, had pushed the pages and paints beneath her quilt and sat trembling, her hands pressed together as if she were praying, as Druscilla jerked the doors open and stood glaring in at her.

"Praying! Praying in the night! What would *you* pray for? And who would hear if you did! And why would you need a candle to pray!" But she had gone away at last, leaving Thursey furious but the truth undiscovered.

Anwin had taught Thursey to cure and grind the colors, and she continued to do it in secret. Dear fat Anwin, where was he wandering now? It must be hard, a monk's life of wandering and begging. Thursey never could believe that he was begging, for truly Anwin worked for his keep, mending the pots as well as a tinker, cobbling the sister's shoes and laying new thatch on the roof. "I must have been up and down this country a hundred times or more, but always and ever there are new souls and new faces. And new joys and new sadnesses." Winter and summer he traveled, just Anwin and his donkey. "One need not be ashamed of dreaming, child. So many are sad because they have ceased to dream. The wonders you know as a child are not meant to die just because you are growing up."

Only once had Anwin interfered when Augusta berated Thursey. "Brat of a coward. Like father like child, and worthless," Augusta had screamed.

"He wasn't a coward. My father wasn't a coward or worthless!"

"Everyone knows it. How could a man as clumsy as he was, who lost two fingers just working in the mill, ever expect to amount to anything or stand up to an enemy?" Augusta taunted.

"Who do you think ran this inn! And he kept *you* decent tempered, which is more than you are now!" Thursey flared. "Anyone can have an accident."

"Any clumsy one. Anyone afraid of the very mill wheel."

"Died a coward," Delilah cut in. "*I* heard he ran from Balkskak's troops when the queen and prince were captured."

Anwin, having listened from the kitchen, had come

into the hall and stared so hard at the three that their gazes dropped in confusion, and Druscilla's face turned red. Anwin said no word, but his furious glare drove the three of them from the hall in silence.

"Pay no attention, child. You can't allow yourself to believe such foolish things."

"I know, Anwin," she mumbled through her tears. "But I don't even know if he's alive or dead. That's what makes me cry."

It had happened so long ago, yet she never stopped hoping her father would come home. Anwin had shaken his head sadly; he would not give her false hope. "Hundreds of men died at Balkskak, child." But when he had gone away, Thursey knew if there were any word of her father, Anwin would seek it out in his travels.

It had been a long desperate battle with Balkskak. When the king's winter palace was attacked, and the queen and the twelve-year-old prince captured, there followed more than three years of warring before the captives were safe again. All the men of the village had been called out at once in a first terrible effort, Thursey's father among them. But the battles raged ceaselessly during the next years, and only occasional news of them reached the village. Thursey had been but a child when her father went away. Three years later when the warring was over, he did not come home again. Nor was there word of him. The returning men did not remember when he was last seen in the confusion of the war. The known dead were mourned over, but those others who were missing seemed to be forgotten. The town, in its delirium over knowing the wounded prince and queen were safe, could talk only of the health of the royal family. For both queen and prince had been dangerously ill with a foreign fever during the whole of their imprisonment and were said to be pale and weak still. The king's attacks had again and again been drawn back with the threat of their imminent deaths.

After the battle they were taken to the far isle of Carthemas, where it was said they might be cured by healers. Now, more than five years after the first battle of Balkskak, it was said the prince was still wasted and suffering, for he had been wounded as well as enervated by the fever.

IT was some days after Thursey sewed the pages of the book of Aschenputtel that she heard the news: the king's party had already left the winter palace and this year they were bringing with them the young prince and the queen. They were expected to arrive well before Easter. The news was carried by a traveling

27

herbalist. He came in the evening riding upon a roan gelding so swaybacked that Thursey stood staring in amazement before she ran to take the man's stirrup and see to his wants. He dismounted like a spider unwinding, so tall and thin he was, and stood looking down at Thursey with a sour expression.

The sisters, peeping through the windows, would perhaps make little of him for he looked poor indeed. Still he was male, and Delilah came simpering out to welcome him. "See to the horse, child, are you dumb? Heat the ale then, get the gentleman's belongings—be off with you!" As the herbalist turned away from Delilah, Thursey saw a bit of a smile on his thin long face, and she grinned boldly back at him. Geddebeuf, his name was, and when he was fed and rested, he took his wares to the center of the village. Sitting on the roan gelding and calling out his wares in a voice like hinges creaking, Geddebeuf drew a crowd around him. "My friends, I am not one of those meager herbalists who stand in front of churches; I am a healer, true and good, and I carry with me medicinals to cure your ills and humors. I bring you wonders from the distant lands, from Apulia and Calabria and Burgundy, from the Forest of Ardennes where wild beasts have been slaughtered that you might benefit from the ointments extracted from them to cure your ills, to cure fevers and coughs and humors and worms, to cure faintness and dispeptics and fallen hair . . ." Thursey listened, enchanted, as his voice rambled on like a creaky trumpet.

Only when the crowd's interest began to wane did Geddebeuf commence to tell of the king's imminent return to the castle. Then the crowd drew close as he spoke of the king's party traveling even now on the high road and of the wonderful Easter ball that was planned.

After supper as Geddebeuf settled his feet on a padded stool and leaned back before the fireplace in the hall, he spoke in even more detail of the coming return of the king, and of the ball the king planned. A ball for the queen and for the young prince, who despite his illness must soon take up his duties as a man. "Ah, they will make a merry time of it, be sure. The king brings with him the finest of poets and minstrels in the land, he brings gleemen and singers and jugglers to cheer the queen, and storytellers with tales of war and love, ribald tales and quaint. He brings musicians who play upon the tambourine and harp, the lute and the rota and the bagpipes, upon the syrinx, the clarion, and the rebec, the psaltery and the sackbut, the gittern, the shalm, and—"

"And the health of the prince is improved?" cut in Augusta with irritation.

"Indeed! The cure is a secret known only to a few of us, and I would have tended the young prince and the queen myself had I not been engaged in other matters."

Delilah laughed scoffingly. "What is the cure, then, herb man?"

"Ah, 'tis made from the milk of a rare kind of goat found only on one island in the whole of the known world, the Isle of Carthemas, and those goats have been brought back in ships by the king. The milk is so rich and wondrous that it, mixed with secret herbs, has made the queen quite rosy, and soon the prince, despite his slow-healing wounds, will be the same. The goats travel with the king's own party and will be stabled right in the castle."

Though the news was interesting, Thursey would have preferred a story. The approaching entourage would throw Delilah and Druscilla into a fit of primping, for many hangers-on would stay at the inn. And, too, the idea of the ailing prince seemed to make the two sisters quite giddy. Druscilla whispered to Delilah, "The dear prince, he will be so weak and pale," and Delilah, sighing, answered, "Oh, the tender care I could give him."

"And the king searches still for the wielder of the sword of Balkskak," Geddebeuf was saying, "for the gallant man who purloined the Balkskakian king's own sword and used it to defend the wounded prince until the king's forward guard found him standing off seven Balkskakian warriors in the palace wine keep where the prince and queen lay bitterly ill . . ." Thursey thought the tale could be told with less pomp; all Gies knew it anyway. But the telling of it seemed to please Geddebeuf and the stepsisters. She thought of the king's party with interest and annoyance mixed. There would be tubs of porridge to boil, loaves to knead so her arms ached thinking of it, troughs of meat and barrels of ale to deal with. And Delilah and Druscilla, busy with demands and bad tempers and very little help, would occupy themselves flirting and getting under foot. Thursey sat silently wondering if she ought to go away. But go away where? And if her father ever returned, he must not find her gone.

She was almost asleep when the herbalist began a story, and Thursey imagined the prince in this story as pale as their own prince must be. Geddebeuf folded lankily over his stool and seemed to gather her in and weave a spell around her so she was lost at once to the tale.

"A king, while hunting in the enchanted swamp, followed a stag, which vanished into a garden in the center of the dark place. The king opened a door into the garden and found himself among trees upon which hung leaves of gold; and there were plants that bloomed diamond flowers. As he picked a rose, a long thread spun out from it and wound around him until he could not move. Then suddenly a dragon appeared, roaring and blowing fire, and it said it would free him only if he promised to bring one of his daughters to be his wife.

"The king returned home sorrowfully, and when his children asked him what the matter was, he told them. The two elder daughters were angry and refused to go to the dragon, saying their father should have stayed captive. But the youngest daughter quickly said that she would go, and the king took her to the dragon as he had promised.

"The dragon met them on the road clad in gold and splendor and escorted them to the palace; and the wedding was very grand indeed. After the wedding the king returned home laden with many gifts.

"Now every day the dragon left the palace, after instructing his wife never to enter a particular room. But one day she did enter it, and there she found a pit, and a young prince at the bottom of it, groaning with

pain. She knew she must rescue him, and when she had thrown him a rope and helped him out, she tended to his wounds. In three weeks' time the prince's health was regained. Then she sent him forth from the palace before the dragon should discover him missing from the pit. She begged him to find and bring to her a large gold chest that could be opened from inside. She could hide in it, and the dragon, thinking her lost, would sell the chest so he would not be reminded of her. . . ."

Thursey was lost in the princess's adventures after the chest was brought, and she sighed with relief when the princess was at last united with the young prince. I wish, Thursey thought, I wish real life could be so sweet.

That night in bed she did not paint pages for the story of "The Dragon," she wrote it down so she could think about it first. Then she took out the thirteen books from beneath her mattress and spread them in front of her. She took up "Tattercoats." She had made the cover out of tiny scraps of cloth to form a true coat of tatters. The background was blue for the sea, the sky, and for the grandfather's tears; the blue ran through every page like a theme of music. White geese marched in the blue borders, and the gooseherd's clothes were blue, his skin as brown as his wooden flute.

"Tattercoats, Tattercoats," the servants chanted. They laughed at her rags and dirt, they laughed at her bare feet and made her run away. They made her hide in the brambles and cry.

No one cared for her, she had no parents, only a grandfather, and he sat all day in the tower and cried rivers of tears. For when Tattercoats was born her mother died, and the grandfather shut himself away and would not see Tattercoats. His white beard grew long and hung out the stone windows like flags waving, and his tears made a salty pool on the floor.

Only the gooseherd was her friend. He played a merry tune for her, he danced for her, he made her laugh and sing.

The little flute appeared on many pages, for it was with the flute that the gooseherd performed his enchantment that helped her marry the prince. In one picture Tattercoats and the prince faced each other on the meadows as the gooseherd played his flute for them. That the gooseherd disappeared after the wedding always made Thursey unaccountably sad.

"Tattercoats, Tattercoats, your grandfather weeps."
She replied, "He has chosen to do so."
"Tattercoats, Tattercoats, the gooseherd is gone."
"The gooseherd, too, has chosen. The sky is blue, the sea is bluer. The sun is warm and I am a princess. For I have married my own true love, and I have found my fortune."

If it occurred to Thursey that there was really no relationship between marrying your own true love and having a fortune showered upon you, she didn't bother about that. In a story you might as well have both, it was make-believe anyway.

But if I had to choose, she thought. If *I* had to choose . . . she stared at her ragged dress hanging from its hook, and her ragged mended sandals on the shelf, then put the books away. How would I ever have such a choice, except in a made-up story?

Chapter Three

TRUMPETS blared. The sharp rhythm of hoofbeats echoed through the village, and the villagers and crofters stood before the shops holding their hats in their hands, their children pushing between their feet. Then they all began to cheer.

First came the archers mounted on bay geldings, then the foreign marshal on a mare the color of storm skies, then the inner marshal, the fat chamberlain, the king's steward, then the chancellor and the clerks, all beautifully mounted. Then the king himself, riding a steed so golden and fine that the sun on him quite dazzled the eye. What a handsome king he was, dark of hair and tall; how straight he sat his stallion.

Behind the king came the carriage of the queen drawn by six gray horses harnessed in a row. A postillion dressed in red livery was mounted on the second horse, holding the reins and brandishing a whip. The wheels of the carriage were carved, the archway of its roof was carved and painted with flowers in gilt and red and blue, and inside one could see tapestries and embroidered pillows. The windows were hung with cloth of blue silk, and the queen herself, her fair hair piled into a high coiffure, smiled and waved and looked in the best of health.

"Though she is still pale," someone said.

"Not very. Look at her smile, like joy itself."

"The loveliest smile in the world." And the people knelt as the queen passed.

"The prince is in there with her, I can see him reclining against the pillows."

"The prince, long live our prince."

"A look—one wave—let him speak to us!"

A figure detached itself from the cushions opposite the queen and a pale, wan face peered out, smiled just barely, and retired.

"He is weak, it has been a long trip."

"But he's the prince, we must see the prince."

"At the ball . . . they say he will lead the ball, that the cure will be complete by Easter." But the crowd's disappointment was great, an ailing prince could not be taken lightly. One day he would be king.

Thursey stared at the pale cheek and felt a twist of pity for the prince, and thought of the tale of the prince in the pit, and the golden box. Then suddenly all such thoughts were driven from her head as she stared at the end of the procession.

Behind the queen's carriage came her ladies, each borne in a low litter, a horse in front and a horse behind carrying it between them, and each litter brightly painted. There were twelve of these, and behind them rode fifty knights dressed in silver mail. But it was not these that made Thursey stare. Nor the clerks that followed, nor the valets nor the grooms.

It was the goats that came last in the procession— and the goatherd.

Those goats were as white as snow. Their curling coats seemed spun of the finest silk; and the billy, in the lead, had horns so long and twisting they might have been the horns of some magical animal. The nannys' smooth faces were the faces of angels. Their unfathomable eyes shone golden and their tiny hooves seemed hardly to touch the ground. One billy and eleven nannys, and one young man to herd them. He was dressed in clean rags and carried a willow staff.

He was a comely young man, and when he passed

Thursey her heart tilted and she gave him a quick, bold smile—partly out of devilment, but mostly because she couldn't help herself. He looked so friendly and nice. His cheeks were tanned and his stride long and easy as if he had spent his life in open places and cared little for false manners. She stared at him and liked him, and she smiled.

And if Thursey's smile came across to the goatherd as the sun rising and the morning dew all glinting gold, no one else seemed to notice. His smile back at her quite dazzled her, and he stopped his goats before her.

"Can you tell me where I can stable my goats? The palace stables will all be full this night, and it is too cold for them on the hills yet; they are not used to it."

"You can stable them at the inn," she said. "I will show you." She turned to lead the way, trying not to think that her stepsisters would have a fit, and that the stalls would all be occupied by the travelers' horses, knowing only that she could not turn him away.

What a dither there had been since the arrival of the Celtic herbalist who had announced the coming of the king's party. Thursey had put fresh straw in all the stalls, cleaned the harness room, turned out all the beds, and baked puddings and cakes and pastries until she felt boiled whole herself with the heat of it and aching in every bone from lifting crocks and barrels and jugs and from the shrill haranguing of Delilah and Druscilla and the stepmother.

But oh, what a heavenly smell had risen and grown in the raftered kitchen, the smell of honey and sugars and cloves, of saffron and sweet wine, and now of great joints roasting on the hearth. The scent, even from the stable yard, was wonderful. Thursey saw the goatherd sniff appreciatively and glance, as if he couldn't help himself, toward the kitchen. He must be hungry, she thought, after such a long journey.

She helped the goatherd—his name was Gillie and his eyes were very blue indeed—bed the goats, turning out a jongleur's mule into the stable yard with the old mare. Then she brought ale and new bread piled with slices of the roasting haunch, and bid Gillie eat behind the stable where Augusta would not see him. Thursey thought that when Augusta and the stepsisters returned from watching the king's company pass, they would have twenty fits at finding goats in the stable. But she did not consider sufficiently that these were the king's own goats.

For, while Gillie might be a common herdboy, the goats were accepted at once by the stepsisters and Augusta as royal creatures. "They're near magical,"

Delilah cried. "They cured the prince—and the queen, too, of course." And the spoiled Magniloquence was pushed out of her stall to make more room for them.

"You will tend these goats carefully while they are in *my* care," Augusta told Gillie. "If anything should happen to the king's goats while they're in *my* stable . . ." Then, to the stepdaughters, "He looks none too clean or responsible." She glanced around as if she expected the chamberlain to be listening, then shot Thursey a commanding glance. "Get them barley and bran mash, girl. Be quick about it. And some vegetables from the table. These are the king's goats you are tending. What are you waiting for?"

Thursey stared and tried to keep from laughing. Ordinarily Augusta would scream that goats stank and chase them out of her yard. She saw Gillie grinning, too, before she turned away.

Late in the night when the crowded inn tables had been filled and filled again, and the platters and mugs and bowls washed several times over, Thursey dried the last dish, turned down the oil lamp, and set a plate of meat and bread before Gillie at the kitchen table. Bawdy songs rang from the dining hall, and she could hear the stepsisters' high laughter. Like cows in clover, Thursey thought, with all those men in there. She stared at Gillie and wished the words of the songs didn't come so plainly into the kitchen.

It didn't seem necessary to talk to Gillie while he ate, the silence was comfortable, if only the singing would cease. There was one song about a Bristol maid that was so bad Thursey rose from her chair and began wiping up the grill, though she had already scoured it thoroughly. "You needn't mind those songs," the goatherd said, "though it is fine of you to blush. I like to see it."

This made Thursey blush all the more, then made her laugh and that made Gillie grin; soon they were laughing so hard they could not even hear the singing.

When they had settled themselves on either side of the fireplace, she poured out ale for him and he told her of Flanders and Bruges, through which they had brought the goats, and of the villages along the high road. He told her how he and the goats had been protected from robbers by the king's own knights, and how, in the early spring when the nannys bore their kids, the kids had been left in the care of the shepherd at the king's southern villa, for they were too young to travel.

Gillie was a gentle lad for all his strapping good looks, and his words were laid down with such care

43

that Thursey could see vividly the hills and the valleys he had traveled, the sudden spring storms, and how, when the rain was over, the fields lay glinting as if a million diamonds had fallen upon them.

"And will you tell me a tale?" she asked boldly. "A story like 'Cendrillon,' like 'Aschenputtel'—have you heard such tales in your travels?"

" 'La Belle Caterina,' " he said at once, his eyes lighting, "from a mummer of Italy. He told it just night before last." He studied her for a long time as if he would ask why she wanted that kind of story. He seemed most intent on the question. But he did not ask. Instead, as a log settled and the fire flared, he commenced the account of a young girl who was sent by her stepmother into the dark swamp woods, "To find a sieve among the wood spirits so she could sift flour to make bread. She was terrified of the evil place, and when she came upon a messenger of the devil, more terrified still." He told how Caterina met next an ogre, and then at last an old man who was kind to her. "The old man helped her to find the cave of the wood spirits, and the spirits led her into a room with cats spinning and weaving and cooking. Pitying the animals, she began to help them in their work, and at last, the cats, upon learning her plight, broke the spirits' spell over

44

her." Gillie told the tale slowly while the embers burned down and the shadows deepened in the corners of the kitchen.

They were so engrossed in each other that neither heard the door open behind them.

Delilah's sharp cry made them turn. She stood in the doorway filling it, surveying the goatherd and the empty plates on the table. She scowled at the ale mug Gillie held; she glowered at the nearly empty honey cake platter (there had been two dozen). "What is the meaning of this! What is this *herder* doing here! What do you mean by letting this filth in my kitchen, it would have been bad enough to give him plate scrapings at the back door! You'll go without your supper for a fortnight, girl, to pay for these takings'" She stormed toward them, her face flaming. "Get out! Get out, out beggar! Catchpenny beggar!" And she shoved at Gillie furiously.

But Gillie stood smiling down at her. Delilah's face turned from red to purple with rage, and Thursey began to giggle. Delilah's eyes grew small with fury, and she drew back her hand to hit Thursey—Thursey could feel the slap before it came.

But it never came.

Gillie caught Delilah's hand before it struck, and

held it firmly in his own. He stared at her for a long time, but said nothing. Then at last he spoke softly, "Don't you hurt her. Not ever. If you ever hurt her I will come back and witch you, old trollop, and you will wish you had never been born." His words were so soft, so measured, and so filled with meaning that a shiver went through the room.

Delilah looked shocked, incredulous, then at last utterly shaken with fury. But she did not speak at all. She seemed unable to. At last she turned and left them, quivering with rage.

"Come on," Thursey said, pulling at him. "Before she . . . I don't know. Before all three of them come back." Though she knew inside herself it wouldn't make any difference, that they could not best Gillie. Not when he stood smiling quietly back at them in that infuriating way.

When they were in the stable yard with the cold night air around them Thursey said, "Could you really do that? Witch her?"

"Wish I *could!*" He grinned at her, scratched his elbow, looked up at the moon, then in at the sleeping animals. When he looked back at Thursey, his eyes were dark and serious. "Well, but the old trollop doesn't know what I can do and what I can't. Maybe she'll have bad dreams."

"SHE'S been sneaking food out of the kitchen!" Druscilla screamed.

"The pots are dirty and the beds aren't changed and the horses aren't curried!" Delilah bellowed.

"That's not true!" cried Thursey, referring only to the last accusations, for she *had* taken food out of the kitchen, and she intended to take more.

"And that mare is getting hay!" cried Delilah.

"She has to eat," Thursey screamed back. "She can't haul the dung cart, and all the fodder and food, too, if she doesn't eat!"

"Shut up!" cried Augusta. "Take her to the fields and let her get her food free, you lazy baggage! Tie her in the fields! Now get to your work and let me hear no more!'

Well, the beds *were* changed, and all the sheets hanging on the line. The pots *were* scrubbed, and all of the horses as clean as freshly washed babies, and the noon meal cooked besides. Druscilla and Delilah could do the serving of it if they wanted any. Thursey turned away in a flurry of anger, and when they had gone she snatched up a basket and began to pack it with new bread and cheese. Defiantly she slipped in a crock of ale. Then she got a rope on the old mare, climbed astride her, not caring a whit that her skirts were hiked up, and set her heels to the mare so hard the mare plunged ahead with surprise. They galloped across the fields, the mare acting almost coltish she was so delighted to be out on such a day. So was Thursey; they breathed the spring air and set their faces into the wind and neither would have paused from racing over the heavily grassed hills, except they finally got to the place they were headed for.

"*Blahhh*," said the nannys. They crowded around the mare, giving her friendly nudges and rubbing against her knobby legs. "*Bahh, bahh*," said the billy, and butted Thursey insistantly when she slid off the mare. The nannys thrust their noses under Thursey's hands and begged to be scratched behind their ears.

Gillie grinned at her and dusted a place for her on the rocks. She tied the mare on a long rope and set the basket down. The breeze came lightly along the hills, and from where they sat they could see the village below them, then on the far hills, the castle rising white. The fields that dropped down below their feet were washed by the wind so the grass went flat in long waves. "The castle always looks so mysterious," she said, awed. "Is it wonderful, living there?"

"It isn't so mysterious when you're there. I'd rather look at it from the hills. It's just—full of people, at least

the servants' parts are, crowded and ordinary. Things should be mysterious, but there's nothing mysterious in the palace."

"*Should* things be mysterious?"

"There's mystery in the hills and in the wind on the grass. And in the stories you like. Isn't life mysterious?"

"My stepmother says life is a weight on our shoulders that we must rise above."

"Old baggage!"

"Gillie!"

"Well isn't she?"

"Yes! Druscilla says life is like a horn of plenty, it won't give anything if you don't squeeze it."

They looked at each other and burst out laughing.

"They think I'm grazing the mare," Thursey said as she served out the bread and cheese.

"Well you are." He watched the mare, amused, as she reached as far as she could after grass, ignoring that under her feet. "What did you tell them yesterday?"

"Nothing. I just disappeared. They were all angry, but I don't care. It's too pretty to stay inside."

"Is that the only reason?"

She blushed, then said defiantly, "I could have taken the mare to the pastures on the other side of the village."

"That would have made me sad."

"Yes. You would have missed your dinner."

"I would have missed you," he said, ignoring her teasing. "I could have my dinner from the cooks at the palace now that I can stable the goats there. The queen herself has given orders that I be fed. But I prefer your cooking."

"And prefer me to steal for you."

His face turned pink at that. "Would you rather not, then?"

"If I would rather not, then I *wouldn't*," she said tartly. "I do it because I like to."

He broke the last piece of bread and poured the ale out equally. "Tomorrow I will ask the cook for a dinner, and you shall be my guest."

"What will we have? Roasted quails and ducklings? Salmon eggs and jellied trout and truffle in wine? Currant cakes and China tea and cream?"

"You shall have," Gillie said, "the king's bread and goat milk."

"The magical goat milk?"

"The same."

"Will it make me beautiful?"

"It cannot. You are already that."

She looked down, flushed, then hurried away to fix the mare's halter.

She would never tell Gillie, but in the night she had dreamed of him; for the three nights since Gillie had come walking down the high road, she had not dreamed of Cinderella stories nor princes, not silks nor silver saddles. She had dreamed of Gillie, of the windy hills and Gillie's warm hand on her own.

He settled back against the hillside and grinned, and began to entertain her with stories of the nobles of the palace, of their foibles and foolishnesses. His sleeves were rolled back and his strong brown arms showed a scar and his hands the roughness of hard work. His eyes, when he did not look at Thursey, looked far down the valley and across at the palace as if he were seeing many things. He made her laugh with his stories, and shocked her sometimes, for she had never thought the nobles of the king's palace could be so foolish.

"How do you know so much about the palace and what goes on in it?"

"Because the servants tell me. Servants take their greatest pleasure in gossip. It's an art and a balm for their own miseries."

"Was it like that when you herded the goats on the Isle of Carthemas?"

"It was after the king's company came. Before that there was only me and my family and the healers. I liked it better that way."

"Then why did you come with the goats clear to Gies castle?"

"Because the king needed me—he is my king after all, in spite of the isolation we lived in. And the prince —the prince needed the goat milk very much."

"Will he be well for the ball? How can anyone be sure?"

"He is mending fast," Gillie said. "The prince will dance at the ball."

"It would be nice for him. He has been away a long time, the people of Gies are anxious to see him."

"Why should they be?"

"Why, he's the prince, Gillie! He'll be king some-day!" She was shocked at Gillie. "He was only a boy when the summer palace was attacked and he and the queen were captured, and he nearly died. He was just barely twelve. They wouldn't even recognize him now. They want to see what he is like—maybe what kind of king he'll be."

Gillie gave her a strange penetrating look. "Perhaps the prince should see what the village is like . . . and if he wants the job."

Gillie was very outspoken. She wondered if he talked so boldly in the castle. Maybe his forwardness came from living too long on Carthemas, removed from the rest of the kingdom. "Why wouldn't he want to rule Gies?"

"I don't know. Would you?"

"I wouldn't know how, I don't think."

"Maybe the prince doesn't either. Or maybe he regrets the loss of his freedom."

"But who is more free than a king?"

"A good king is beholden to his subjects. Only a bad king makes free to do as he pleases." Then he grinned at her. "There was a ballad last night. They let the servants stand at the door to the great hall and listen. It was the kind of story you are fond of—you are like her, Thursey. Like Catskin. You have the stepsisters, and a stepmother as grisly as any of those . . ."

Did he see so plainly, then, that she felt one with those others sometimes? "And my father, too, has gone away," she said quietly. "Though in the stories those girls know where their fathers are."

"Was it the war, then? The battles of Balkskak?"

"Yes. He went with the rest of the village, but he didn't come back. No one seemed to have seen him when the last battle was over, all they could talk about was the prince and queen being saved and the sword of Balkskak. I can understand that but—but you'd think someone would know if he died or—or where he is."

"No one could tell you anything?" There was a strong line along Gillie's jaw that hardened when he was concerned.

"No one except my stepmother. She said she heard—
I don't believe it—that he died a coward and didn't
fight for the king. That he had run off and that was
why no one had seen him."

"Why would she say such a thing?"

"She says he was clumsy and a coward because he
was crippled working in the mill, but I don't . . ."

"Anyone can be injured," Gillie said softly. "She's
an old bear anyway. Crippled how?"

"He lost two fingers in the mill. She said that happened because he was afraid, and not bold in the way
he handled the grinding wheel, but . . ." She stopped
talking, for Gillie looked so strange.

He seemed almost not to see her for a few moments;
then his look changed, and he grinned. "Will you hear
the tale now? The story of Catskin that the Irish min-
strel sang? Though I won't sing it as he did."

"Oh yes," she said and settled down to listen, watching Gillie with curiosity.

He told her of the magic filly who watched over
Catskin, and of the three enchanted gowns the filly
gave her, that could be hidden in walnut shells. . . .
"Catskin wandered alone in the dark forest until she
came to a palace where she was taken in as a serving
maid. . . ." As the tale unfolded, Thursey could see the
prince clearly, for he looked like Gillie. "And when

55

Catskin shook the walnut shell over herself, the dress of silver and silk fitted to her at once. . . ." Thursey looked down at her own dress, patched and faded, and felt her hair all tangled from the wind. Look at me, she thought, distressed. What must Gillie think!

For Gillie was so handsome, his brown hair curling close to his forehead and his cheeks tanned from the sun, his calloused hands strong and yet so gentle with the goats. How can he even look at me, she thought. And all of a sudden she knew she wanted very much for Gillie to like looking at her.

She was afraid he might guess how she felt, and more afraid he might not—terrified that he could never feel the same.

When the story was finished, he gave her a solemn glance. "And just as Catskin went to the ball, and Cendrillon, and Aschenputtel, so must you. The ball that will be given soon in the palace; I've heard talk of it in the kitchens. The servants say one is held each year. Have you never gone?"

She shook her head.

"Then you must go this year dressed in a fine gown as it is done in the stories."

She sat staring at him. "Me, Gillie? I don't belong at the ball."

"As much as Cinderella did."

"But they are only stories; they're not things that can happen." She studied him for a long time. He did not seem to be making a joke.

"It's what you dream, Thursey. You should do what you dream of doing, else where is the good in dreaming?" A nanny nuzzled against him, and he stroked her absently. "Every year your sisters go, I'll wager. And every year they make you stay at home, isn't that so?"

She colored, for it was true.

"Then this year you must go, too."

"I can't go, I have no dress to wear. They would stop me anyway." Couldn't he see that the ball didn't matter any more? Now that she knew Gillie, dreaming of princes had no meaning.

"We will get you a dress with magic, just as in the stories," he said seriously.

"But they're only stories, Gillie. Magic isn't *real*."

"We will make it real."

She could only stare, perplexed.

THURSEY went home slowly, with the old mare taking her time, for she liked coming out better than going back, and she was full to bursting with sweet grass and would have preferred a nap in the field. Thursey put her head down on the old mare's neck as they walked, but the mare, stopping suddenly and on purpose, almost dumped her over her head. She looked around at Thursey with an evil gleam in her eye, then went on, walking faster now and nodding her head knowingly. "If you're so smart," Thursey growled at her, "why don't you tell me what he was talking about! *What* kind of magic? And why does he want me to go? What if I *married the prince*! That would serve him right, stupid Gillie!"

The mare stumbled on a stone and nearly spilled Thursey again, and when Thursey pulled her up and kicked her, she broke into a fast gallop, switching her tail as if she might buck. She raced for home with glee (though she was well beyond the years for that sort of foolishness) and stopped only when she reached her own gate.

Thursey slid off and turned the mare into the yard. "Old hoyden! You've no more dignity than a trollop in a street fight! And you've not answered my question. *Why* would he . . ." The mare had turned and was looking right at Thursey, and a thought occurred to Thursey so suddenly that she stood staring back, speechless, while she examined it. "Maybe . . ." Thursey said, "Oh, maybe he . . . maybe he isn't thinking of himself! Maybe he's just thinking about me, maybe he just wants *me* to be happy!"

Chapter Four

THREE figures came riding down from the palace, their coats red against the hills and their trumpets blaring. The villagers stopped cobbling and weaving and tinkering and gossiping and crowded into the square.

The two trumpeters' horses pawed at the cobbles. The herald stood up in his stirrups and held up a document to read, and the villagers were quiet.

"By royal order of his most revered highness, the King of Gies, hear ye this announcement:

Upon the Sunday of Easter, on the day of our Lord, the doors of the palace will open, the musicians will play, and the King will welcome you, each one, peasant and freeman, serf, crofter, villein, lord, steward, seneschel, bailiff, and reeve, and all of your ladies, to the

59

King's annual ball, the spring ball to ensure good crops and good harvest and prosperity upon the land. This most important ball since the battles of Balkskak, the ball to welcome the queen and prince home to Gies castle."

The villagers cheered and Thursey thrilled at the fine sound of the words. The trumpets blared again, and the herald dismounted and pulled out another parchment and began to make the lists.

Every year it was the same, the names of all those who would attend were given to the herald and set upon the parchment. And every year it was the same, Augusta stumped forward in her black habit, gave her own name first, then that of Druscilla, then Delilah. But never Thursey.

Only this year it was *not* the same.

Augusta stumped forward and gave her own name. Then Druscilla. Then Delilah. Then she turned to go.

"Is that all?" asked the herald.

"All!" said Augusta over her shoulder.

"*Not all!*" said a voice from the crowd.

Thursey stood on her toes to look. Stepping out from behind a tiny donkey was a monk as round and cheery as one could imagine. His brown robe was dusty and

wrinkled and his tonsure seemed grayer, but Anwin's smile was just as merry as ever.

"Not all, lady," repeated Anwin. "You have one more daughter who is old enough to dance at the ball."

Augusta had stopped dead, and now she turned upon Anwin with fury in her eyes.

The herald frowned at her. "Is this so, woman? The King wants *every* girl, particularly this year."

"She was too young before," Augusta said glibly. "I was just about to give her name when . . ." she glared at Anwin.

"What is it then, woman?" The herald did not seem enchanted with Augusta.

"It is Thursey!" Augusta spat defiantly, and now her glare had settled on Thursey herself with such hatred that Thursey trembled. Oh, what good would it do to have her name on the lists? Augusta would think of some way to keep her home and would be all the more cruel because of it. Still it was kind of Anwin to try, to stand up for her so. And how good it was to see him. She grinned and stepped forward, but Anwin was addressing Augusta.

"Have you lodging, mistress?"

Augusta gave him a black look. "Yes, lodging," she said shortly and hatefully, and turned away from him. She had not the courage to refuse the monk, though she would make his stay as miserable as she dared.

"STABLE the donkey then," Augusta told Thursey when they were home, "but feed it straw! And see that that monk mends the pots for his keep, the lazy good-for-nothing, and puts new thatch on the roof. I can't run a charity for every beggar and catchpenny in the country!"

Thursey put the little donkey in a clean stall and gave him such a pile of hay she could hardly see him on the other side of it. And when her work was done, she raced out to the hills and found Anwin pottering about among some tansy, picking bits here and there and humming to himself and to the bees that accompanied him.

He took her hands and stood staring at her, and it occurred to Thursey with a shock that she no longer had to look up to meet Anwin's eyes. She was taller than Anwin by several inches. "You've grown," he said, smiling. "You've grown into a young lady."

"I . . . maybe not quite a lady, Anwin. Augusta says I'm not. Have you news for me of my father?"

"Yes, child," he said softly. "But I was hoping you wouldn't ask me right off. It does not pleasure me to bring it."

She stared at him and could say nothing.

He remained silent, looking so unhappy.

When at last she found her voice, it was no more than a croak. "He is dead, then, Anwin? Is my father dead?"

"Yes, child, he is dead. But he died, I am sure from the information I have, among the king's troops that stormed into Balkskak castle."

She turned away from Anwin and stood looking out over the windy fields. She thought she felt her father close to her.

Died among the king's troops as they stormed into Balkskak castle. Died and would never come home again. Died . . . he would not come home, not ever. How much she had counted on that, on seeing her father again. She turned at last to Anwin, and he put his arms around her and held her for a long. time.

My father died storming Balkskak castle, she thought over and over and tried not to think: He will not come home to Gies ever.

When at last she had calmed herself, Anwin said softly, "There was a goatherd here. He spoke of you and has your dinner for you. He said there was plenty for three, but I . . ."

"Oh," she said, pulling her thoughts back from the blackness, "Oh, do come Anwin. You'll like him." It would do no good to pine by herself. She took Anwin's hand and began to lead him up over the hills.

Gillie was settled in the lee of some boulders where the sun hit warm. He spread out currant cakes and lamb pie, blackberries and tea with heavy cream, China cakes and trifle.

"How did you ever get it all?" Thursey said in amazement, trying to put the sadness away from her for the sake of the other two.

"I made a friend of the cook."

"Is she young and beautiful?" Thursey said, grinning.

"She's old and wrinkled and kind."

Thursey sat down on the grass with her feet tucked under her, and the monk settled more slowly, to recline against the warming stone, his boots stuck out comfortably from under his brown habit. And in spite of the quantity of food he consumed, he began adroitly to winnow out the story of the goats and how the prince and queen had come to the Isle of Carthemas to be cured, and how Gillie was set to tend the flock.

"The king brought the queen and prince, himself, with only a few trusted servants, long before the royal party came," Gillie said quietly. "And the queen and prince were taken to the hills where the sun is strong, to rest in its warmth and be treated by the healers with our goat's milk and cheeses and herbs. It is a wild, bonny place, Carthemas, and the air is clear and pure."

"The prince must have been badly wounded when he was made captive," Anwin said. "A wound that took so long to heal."

"An ugly wound, and the sickness and fever seemed to prevent it from healing. An ugly battle too, it is told," Gillie said easily.

Anwin leaned back sleepily against the boulders. "And where were you during the war with Balkskak, young Gillie? On the Isle of Carthemas all that time?"

"Carthemas didn't even know there was a war until long after Gies's summer palace was freed, and the prince and queen brought half dead across the sea to rest there."

"They say he is very weak still," Anwin said. "That he hardly showed his face when the king's party entered the village."

"I saw him wave," Thursey said. "A thin, pale boy inside the curtains."

"The prince is a man grown," Gillie said shortly.

"Yes, but thin all the same."

"Wait until the night of the ball; the prince has vowed to dance until dawn. I think," Gillie said, studying Thursey, "that he will find you a winsome partner. Maybe he will dance with no other."

Her face turned warm with embarrassment.

"What will you wear?" Anwin asked softly. "For Gillie's right, child, you'll be the loveliest lass at the ball."

"Oh, Anwin, I can't go. They will never let me."

"I saw the herald ride down," Gillie said. "Was he announcing the ball?"

"Yes, and Anwin made Augusta give my name for the lists."

"Then you must go. They say the king commands that all on the lists must attend."

"If Augusta has to let me, then she'll dress me in something horrid." She stroked the silken white coat of the nanny beside her. "Besides I—I truly don't want to go." Why couldn't Gillie understand that to dance with a prince was not what she wanted at all.

"Yes, you do," Gillie said heartlessly. "I can see it in your eyes. I told you I would help you with a bit of magic, and I will. Just you wait and see." And he winked at Anwin.

"YOU should get a beating," fumed Augusta, "but there isn't time. Get those chests in the hall open, we

67

must have the silks out for suitable gowns. Hurry!"

"But I thought—"

"The chests!" screamed Augusta.

"BUT I THOUGHT THEY HAD GOWNS," Thursey screamed back. "I made them just after Christmas, their gowns for the King's ball!"

"Wrong color," Augusta said shortly. "Delilah hates green, and lavender makes Druscilla look bilious. You haven't any taste; you made a botch of it, and now it is to do over and not a minute to spare! GET THOSE CHESTS OPEN!"

"But *I* didn't pick out the colors, *they* did!" Thursey didn't expect an answer to that. She flounced into the hall and began banging open the heavy oaken chests that lined one wall. If she were going to get a tongue-lashing, then she might as well be nasty enough to earn it. Besides, Augusta couldn't do much to her, or there would be no one to sew the new dresses. She began lifting the laces and the satins, the voiles, the silks of amethyst and scarlet and melon, the taffetas of cerise and amber, out of the heavy chests and laying them across the great trestle tables.

Then she brought a looking glass, and the sisters tried one fabric and another, making Thursey hold each piece to each of them while they preened and studied themselves from all angles.

Nothing seemed to suit. "Bring that one" Delilah ordered. "No, *that* one—I can't stand *that*. Why can't you find anything really lovely, all of these are rags!"

Finally Druscilla settled on a cloth of gold that made her skin look quite yellow, and Delilah chose a bolt of bright red satin that Thursey thought singularly unflattering. Augusta chose black silk, as Thursey knew she would, and she wondered why Augusta's old black silk wouldn't do. But of course. They were going to keep her so busy she would have no time to make a dress for herself.

"And what will I wear to the ball?" she asked as innocently as she could manage.

"Wear?" cried Augusta. "You? *You* won't have time to make yourself a dress; you'll have to wear something of Delilah's!" She turned on her heel and left the hall, Druscilla directly behind her and Delilah behind her. Thursey began to fold the yards and yards of silk and put them in the chests.

"TRY them on," said Delilah, flinging down half a dozen worn gowns before Thursey. Thursey had been fitting the red satin dress to Delilah and the cloth of gold dress to Druscilla. (Sewing for the two of them was like making a sword sheath and a mattress cover, but with more difficulties.)

69

Thursey tried on the dresses one by one, while Druscilla and Delilah and Augusta sat about on the beds and made comments.

Delilah's clothes were like tents on Thursey, tents equipped with ruffles. The shoulders drooped down to her elbows, and the bodices draped in lumpy layers down her front. "You could take that one in a little and it would be quite charming," said Augusta of a bile green creation. "The color is very good." It was a terrible color. It made the shadows under Thursey's eyes (she had sewn all night) go purple.

Druscilla and Delilah agreed that it was the very dress. "It makes you look quite sophisticated," said Druscilla.

"The men always gazed at me in that dress," Delilah said.

When Thursey looked at herself in the mirror, the reflection made her gag.

"The very thing," said Augusta with finality and sent Thursey off to get on with her sewing.

Thursey flung the bile green dress into the broom cupboard and began to sew the hem of the black silk, jabbing and jabbing her needle as if she were jabbing it into her stepmother. But soon enough her temper cooled, for Anwin came to sit in the kitchen, and she made tea for them and cut a little cake. "The roof's all thatched," said Anwin. "How is the sewing coming?"

"I worked all night," said Thursey bitterly. "It's not much fun to sew for those three."

"Like the silk purse and the sow's ear," observed Anwin. "And have you begun a ball gown for yourself, child?"

"You should see what they gave me to wear!" She opened the broom closet and held the bile green dress up to herself.

"Oh my," said Anwin. He studied it a long time. "Oh, how very dreadful." Then he began to laugh. Soon they were both laughing.

"But what *will* you wear?" he asked finally, pouring out more tea.

"I don't know, Anwin. Gillie said—he said he would bring magic to make a dress, but I—"

"If he said it," Anwin interrupted, "then surely he will do it, child."

But Thursey didn't know how he could. And the thought of the ball, and of the bile green dress, and Gillie's impossible promise of magic quite saddened her somehow. Late at night when her eyes were red from sewing, she crawled into bed and, instead of falling asleep at once, took out the painted books.

Their colors, and the hope in the stories, lifted her spirit, and she sat reading for a long time by candlelight, until she fell asleep at last with the books scattered on the quilt and the candle burnt to nothing.

IT was a week later, and very early in the morning that she woke to a light tapping on the back door. "Who is it?" Thursey whispered, having come awake at once.

"It's Gillie. May I come in?"

She arose quickly and opened the door to see dawn streaking the dark sky and Gillie carrying a package.

"What is it?" she asked, taking the outthrust bundle.

"Can I come in?"

She backed away to let him in and blushed faintly, because in the dream from which she had just awakened he had been kissing her. "I'll make some tea," she whispered, stirring up the ashes and putting on some wood. "But what is in the package?" She began to slice the bread.

"Come and open it."

The wrapping was of purest linen tied with silver cord. When she had untied the cord and folded the wrapping back, she could not believe what shone up at her.

It was silver cloth embroidered with flowers in shades

of blue and red and the petals and stems of gold. It was like a spring day, that cloth, like the sun on a delicate garden.

Thursey held it up, and Gillie looked at her with admiration, then brought the mirror.

"Oh Gillie!"

The bits of turquoise and azure in the flowers caught the color of her eyes and made them bluer. (If they *could* be any bluer, thought Gillie.) And the flowers of tangerine and rose, the silver and gold, glowed richly. "Oh Gillie! Wherever did you get it? What kind of magic could you have used? You haven't stolen it from the palace?"

"I haven't stolen it," he said. "But do you like it?"

"It's the most beautiful thing I ever saw. I'll be afraid to touch it with the scissors."

"You will make a lovely dress of it. You'll be the sensation of the ball." And then he took her hand and kissed her gently.

Thursey cut the beautiful cloth late at night, laying it out on the kitchen table. She trembled with fear that she would ruin it or that her stepmother would come in. But before she ever laid scissors to it she made herself a model, cut out of the rough cotton from which she made her underclothes and nightgowns, and stitched hastily to see that the fit would be right. Only then did she begin on Gillie's gift. And as she sewed, she paused again and again to hold a bit of the cloth up to herself before the looking glass. She sewed by candlelight each night until dawn began to come, then she would fold the dress carefully and lay it under her mattress.

And in the daytime she worked on the other three dresses. Though, like a canny fox, she took her time over the sisters' gowns, for she knew very well that if she finished too soon, they would find something else to prevent her from working on a dress of her own. (The chests in the hall had been mysteriously locked after the sisters had chosen their fabric.) How they must have snickered at the thought of Thursey trying to alter Delilah's bile green satin.

"I HEARD," Druscilla said, "from a carter who heard it from a page in the palace, that the Sword of Balkskak will lie on display in the great hall the night of the ball."

"What for? Why would they put a sword in the ballroom!" Her stepmother scoffed.

"Because it saved the prince! Because it's a symbol of the prince's safety and return home," she said in a manner that implied she knew more than anyone, including Augusta.

"You'd better watch your tongue—" Augusta began.

"Oh, how romantic," Delilah interrupted. "The very sword, there in the ballroom for all of us to see and touch, just as we'll see the prince. I heard," she whispered conspiratorially, "that maybe they've found the man who wielded it. . . ."

At once Augusta's expression turned scheming. "If the prince is too pale and weak to wed one of you, perhaps such a man . . ."

"Would make a good husband," Druscilla finished. "Oh yes, I could love such a man as that . . ."

Sickened at the three of them, Thursey turned away to finish laying the tables. She tried to hide a yawn, but sharp-eyed Druscilla saw her. "What are you yawning for? You look quite done for sleep—look at her! What are you doing at night that you don't get your sleep, not praying, surely! Slipping out with that dirty herd-boy, likely."

"Sewing!" Thursey said defiantly. Well, she had been sewing, but on her own gown in the wee hours. "Your gowns take a long time, with my other work in the day."

"And with slipping off to the hills to who-knows-what kind of behavior!" Delilah put in. "And that monk . . ."

Thursey turned deliberately and pushed through the door to the kitchen. She was afraid she would lose her temper if she stayed. Dead for sleep, and irritable, she was in no mood for the sisters' haranguing. Alone in the kitchen, she sighed and wondered if she *could* finish all four gowns in time for the ball.

But on the morning of the ball, she sewed the last stitch in her own gown, and the other three hung nearly ready for the stepsisters and Augusta. She was heavy-eyed and dull when dawn streaked the sky, but she laid her needle aside, stripped off her night dress, and lifted the beautiful garment over her head.

She stood before the mirror and gazed at herself. The skirt of the gown made a wide arc, hanging in lovely folds and nipping in at her waist delightfully. The bodice was low and showed her curves just enough, but not wantonly. The little sleeves were no more than whispers. The colors of the fabric shone in the candlelight as if the fabric was lit from within: a tender glowing brightness. Thursey sighed with wonder at the reflection that looked back at her. How she wished that Gillie would come tapping now.

After breakfast she washed Delilah's hair in rainwater and was curling it up on bits of cloth when Druscilla began screaming frantically from the hall below. Thursey thought she had found the gown tucked beneath her mattress, and she raced down in panic, Delilah and Augusta pushing at her heels.

They found Druscilla standing in the middle of the hall, her head raised, screaming at the top of her lungs. When Augusta started toward her, she stopped screaming, stuck out her hands, and cried, "Stop! You'll mash them!"

Augusta came charging on, took one step where the rushes were thin, and fell flat on her backside.

All around Augusta's sprawling form, strewn among the rushes, were little glints of light.

It was Druscilla's pearls. She had broken her string of pearls.

"Seventy-two," said Augusta, getting slowly up and rubbing her bruises. "Seventy-two exactly. And the string cannot be restrung without every one of them." She turned toward Thursey and scowled. "What are you waiting for?"

Thursey got down on her hands and knees and began searching out the pearls from among the rushes. When she had found twenty-four, she could see no others, and she began picking up the rushes themselves to clear the floor. I'm like Aschenputtel, she thought. For Aschenputtel's stepmother, just before the ball,

threw a dish of lentils into the ashes and made Aschenputtel pick up every one. But, Thursey thought, the
white bird came to help her. There's no white bird
for me.

"All seventy-two," repeated Augusta and turned on
her heel to leave.

"But . . . but . . . but . . ." sobbed Druscilla, pointing
to the corner of the hall.

"What *now!*" bellowed Augusta. "What are you
pointing at?"

"Down that mousehole," cried Druscilla. "One went
down that mousehole!"

When Augusta had departed, ranting, Druscilla dissolved in another pool of tears, and Delilah sat down
on a chair while Thursey continued to crawl about on
her hands and knees seeking pearls among the rushes.

Soon she had found forty-nine.

"Look harder," grumbled Delilah.

Then fifty-six.

"Keep looking," sobbed Druscilla.

Then sixty-seven.

"Move more rushes," advised Delilah.

And finally she had seventy-one pearls safely in her
apron.

"Now the mousehole," said Delilah. "Put your hand
in."

She tried, but it wouldn't fit.

"You're not trying hard enough," sobbed Druscilla.

"You will find that pearl," said Augusta stalking in again, "or you will not go to the ball."

Finally Thursey, failing to dig the pearl out or even to see it with her eye to the mousehole, went to sit sadly in the stables with Anwin. "I can't go to the ball, then," she said. "I'll never wear Gillie's dress. Augusta says the string can't be finished without it, and Druscilla can't go without the pearls, and I can't go if she can't!"

"In a mousehole," Anwin mused. "I have heard talk involving magic and a mouse."

"Oh, Anwin," Thursey said with disgust. "Don't talk like Gillie! Magic can't help me now."

"Magic got your dress, didn't it?"

"Gillie brought the material."

"But how do you know he didn't get it by magic? And even if magic won't help you, maybe the mouse can help."

"What do you mean?"

"Think about the hole," said Anwin. "Think about it like a mouse would, think about what it is like to be in there."

"All right," she said hopelessly. She thought about the little mouse going down into the hole, dark and warm, climbing down and down until he reached—

79

what? A warm dark tunnel? A little cave with a soft bed made of lint and feathers? It must be below the floor then, his bed.

And below the floor was—what? What would his walls be made of?

Thursey scrambled up, grabbed a trowel and ran round the outside of the inn to the corner of the hall.

There she began to dig. And pretty soon, when she had dug the dirt away from under the corner of the hall floor, the trowel pushed suddenly into an opening and she looked in to see a nest of lint and thread, and, lying to one side, Druscilla's pearl.

"Now child," said Anwin when Thursey had returned the pearl and restrung all seventy-two onto a linen thread, "Put on your ball gown for me, for I will not be here to see you dressed in it tonight."

"But Anwin, you have to stay for the ball. And it's Easter, you won't travel on Easter."

Anwin shook his head. "I'll be on the high road among the silence and the hills on Easter day, child. I don't take to all the pomp and fuss of the king's ball—especially at Easter when I would rather be alone with my own prayers."

She dressed in the gown for him and pinned up her hair, and Anwin took from his pocket a pair of silver

shoes that fitted her exactly. "And how will you ride to the ball? In the carriage with your stepsisters?"

"I'll ride the old mare, I guess."

"With your skirts hiked up?"

"I will. I don't trust what Augusta and those two would think of to do to me between here and the castle, Anwin."

He laughed, thinking she was right. "You could perhaps slip off on Augusta's old sidesaddle, though. I've seen it in the harness room."

"I'd feel a fool, Anwin. I only know how to ride like a boy."

The old man grinned broadly, thinking of her riding with her skirts hiked up, to the castle. "Well you are too beautiful for it to matter. And wearing that gown, no one will notice how you got there. Now let me see the books you have done while I've been away."

She brought them out, and while she stitched on the hem of Druscilla's gold dress, he examined each one attentively. "Child, oh, child," he said at last, "How lovely. They're beyond my wildest imaginings."

"Which do you like best?"

"It's hard for me to say. One of these two, but I'm not sure which." He held up the story of the gooseherd, and "Liisa and the Prince." "Gillie is like the gooseherd. He, too, has made magic so you can go to the ball."

"Oh—oh, no, Anwin! Not Gillie!"

And then he saw what he had done, for the goose-herd had gone away forever. He put his arm around her. "But Gillie won't disappear, he's far too real for that, child. Here now, here now. . . ."

When she had quieted, he continued examining the books. The boldest, "Liisa and the Prince," he looked at again and again. There was red for the fire that Liisa carried in the skull and for the burning pit. And black for the dark forest and for the ogress, black for the lamb that strayed. White for the linen dress Liisa put on, white for the spilled milk she must pick up. Anwin read some of the pages aloud, quite engrossed. "The ogress spat in the face of Liisa's mother, and said, 'My body to you, yours to me,' and they were changed about. But only Liisa knew." He smiled and examined the pages, then read the last lines, "The prince built a pit of burning tar and the ogress and her daughter fell into it, into the fire, and that was the end of them. And Liisa heard the spirit of her mother whisper, 'Now I shall rest for I know you are happy at last.'

"Lovely," Anwin said. "Lovely. Has Gillie seen your books?"

"Oh no, he would think them childish."

"Are you sure?"

"I—I don't know, Anwin. Wouldn't he?"

But Anwin only smiled.

Chapter Five

I HEARD it in the brewer's," Augusta said. "The king *has* placed the Sword of Balkskak on a dais in the ballroom."

"*I* heard," Delilah simpered among clouds of dusting powder and perfume, "*I* heard they *know* who wielded it at Balkskak!"

"Why would they wait until now?" Augusta said with disdain.

"For drama!" Druscilla said haughtily. "So it can be announced at the ball. I wonder who . . ." Her bulging eyes lit with selfish interest.

"It must be someone in the king's own company," Delilah ventured. "If it was a village lad, we'd have heard . . ."

"Knights have been riding in all week for the ball," Augusta reminded them. "Maybe they did just find out," she said in a rare fit of reasonableness. "Though," she added, "it's probably just a trumped-up story done for show, to make the ball more interesting. Get on with your dressing. Do you want to be late?"

Late? Thursey thought. They've been at the unguents and facials and footbaths ever since Easter services this morning. She finished the ironing, took up the comb, and began on Delilah's curls. Delilah's red satin stretched tightly, as she would have it, over her bulges, and the flesh that emerged from her low neckline was startling. At the other dressing table, Druscilla fastened on her pearls. Her hair, which she had done herself, was piled in an arrangement that resembled nothing Thursey could think of.

"And now," said Delilah as Thursey combed out the last curl, "now the red slippers, and that will top it all off."

But when Thursey had brought the slippers, Delilah screamed with rage, "There's a hole in the toe of one, and there's a hole in the heel of the other! A mouse!" she bellowed. "A mouse has been at my slippers!"

That mouse! thought Thursey. Some kind of magic that mouse is!

"Get another pair," commanded Augusta, bearing down on Thursey. "Get another pair at once!"

"But where?"

"The cobbler, stupid! Be off!"

"But it's Easter, his shop will be closed. He couldn't make shoes before the ball anyway, there isn't time."

"He *must*! Tell him he must. Now be off." Thursey pelted down the stairs, and Augusta's shout followed her, "Tell him by order of the King!"

Thursey nearly choked on that as she fled across the yard.

Delilah poked her head out the window, "No shoes," she yelled, "you little baggage, and there'll be no ball for you!" Thursey tore down the village street with her anger rising like a tide, to pound on the cobbler's door.

But when the cobbler came shuffling to unlock for her and had heard what she wanted, he only looked at her irritably. "I can't," he said, observing the chewed slippers. "I can't possibly, there simply isn't time."

"But what am I to do?"

"What about the monk at the inn? That old fellow can cobble—but no one can make a pair of slippers before the ball tonight."

"Could you make *one* slipper?"

"Well I guess . . . he began hesitantly.

"Then if I could find Anwin—he left today, but a little donkey can't go so far—if I can find Anwin he could make the other! Oh, *could* you try?"

"I'll try," said the cobbler, and took up Delilah's old slipper for a pattern.

Off she went, round the cobbler's and down the street and round again on the dirt path kicking up streamers of dust and onto the old mare's back, hardly taking time to tie the halter round her head properly. Then out the gate and down the high road following the little donkey footprints (no other donkey in the kingdom had such tiny feet). Running full tilt, the old mare turned her head around twice to stare at Thursey, as surprised as you please.

When she saw Gillie on a knoll, she could only wave at him, though all the goats bleated, and Gillie shouted, "Thursey, Thursey, wait . . ." But she was gone, the wind catching at her hair.

On they went with the hoofprints always ahead of them. Oh, how far he had gone. The mare clattered through a dry stream and over a little hill and there was not a soul about. Thursey began to wonder about robbers. They pelted past the dark marsh and Thursey thought she caught the scent of roses once; then at last she saw Anwin beside a brook eating the bread and cheese she had packed for him earlier. She handed him the shoe and told him the story in one breath.

Anwin said nothing. He dug into his bag, pulled out his cobbler's tools, found a bit of red leather, and set to work.

"Oh Anwin," she whispered, "you can."

"I can try," he said. "I can only try."

By the time Thursey reached the village once more, dusk was falling, and she had met the first carriages on the road, the horses shining and the ladies glittering in their ball gowns. The old mare was done, sweating and blowing. Thursey jumped off her in front of the cobbler's shop and found him just finishing the slipper. She sped away with it, turned the mare into the stable yard, and pounded up the stairs with the slippers in her hand, then down again to rub the sweat from the mare and harness Magniloquence. "And be sure you polish the harness," Druscilla flung after her. She had received no thanks for the slippers. The three had only glared at her and wondered what took her so long. "You'll have to hurry to get the carriage ready," called Delilah.

"You'd better put some supper on," shouted Augusta. "And heat the ale."

"They won't serve any food at the palace until midnight," complained Delilah. "These slippers are awfully tight, they hurt my toes."

When the carriage was ready and the old mare had

been rubbed down so she wouldn't take cold, Thursey went into the kitchen thinking, Cold lamb and bread should be enough. And ale.

And there they were, Delilah's fat figure in red, Druscilla's thin one in gold, and Augusta a square black box. The doors to Thursey's bed had been flung open and they were crowded around it. The mattress was turned back, and the beautiful gown lay across it.

"Where did she get it?" screamed Delilah.

"You can't let her wear it!" cried Druscilla.

Their three glares of hatred turned full upon Thursey.

"No matter where she got it," said Augusta, picking up the dress, "she will never wear it." She held it up before her so the colors glowed, smiled for a long moment, and then she ripped it in two down the middle.

Then she ripped out the little sleeves.

Then she tore each of the pieces in half, and in half again, and the threads, as they parted, snagged and pulled across the cloth—it seemed Augusta's passion would leave nothing at all, not a remnant. When she had spent herself at last, she flung the tangle onto the floor and took herself out, her daughters marching haughtily behind her.

They mounted into the carriage behind Magniloquence, forgetting their supper in their wrath, and trotted down the lane to the high road, heads erect and uncompromising, and up the high road toward the palace.

Thursey went out finally to the old mare, her eyes swollen from weeping. The poor dress was beyond repair, and she could only go to the mare for comfort. For spirit comfort and for creature comfort, for someone gentle to be alone with, this loneliest of nights.

But the mare was gone.

Her stepsisters had left the gate open. Oh, how cruel and horrible they were! Thursey would have dissolved into weeping again, but this turn of events made her so mad that she pounded the fence with her fist, then started out after the mare.

She had left the torn dress on her bed, closing the doors across it and unable to look again. She felt so bad for Gillie. She didn't know what she would say to him, it was as if she had betrayed a sacred trust that he had put in her. He had given her a gift that must have cost him something very dear, and she had let it be destroyed.

She searched and searched among the hoofprints on the high road, but so many horses had gone along it that she had to walk a long way, first in one direction, then in the other, before she could locate the familiar broken-hooved trail. Then she hurried along it, alone, up the high road.

As she followed the mare's hoofprints, the dark began to come down so she thought she must lose the trail soon. She studied the darkening hills for a white form. But even if she saw one, it could be Gillie's goats and not the mare at all.

But Gillie would not have them out so late. He would be at the palace watching the ball from some dark place where the servants were allowed to peek out. What would he think when he did not see her dancing in the gown he had given her?

Once she saw a bit of white and ran over the hills to it, but it was only a rock. Soon it was so dark she could no longer find the hoofprints.

Then the moon began to send up its light before itself, a pale gleam behind the hills, that grew slowly. It threw shadows across the hills, then made their round faces grow lighter. Now she could see the mare's trail a little, and she hurried faster.

Then the moon itself came, a sliver. Then it was more than a sliver, and the hoofprints were etched sharply upon the whitened road. Then the moon pulled itself up on top the last hill, tore away and hung suspended, and the hills themselves were bathed in its icy light. Thursey searched the landscape, but she was entirely alone.

Now on her left was a copse of dark trees, and she thought of robbers. She tried to think, instead, how the carriages would look arriving at the ball. They would be lined along the drive, and from each would step down gentlemen with lace at their cuffs and swords hanging at their sides and ladies in lovely gowns. Were there footmen to take the horses' heads? But of course there would be. A shadow on her left seemed to have moved. Now it was still, though, and she went on, listening. Nothing stirred behind her. On her right was the swamp now, the moon caught the shallow water and the mud flats into a silver lake. What was that, far out on the swamp path? It was white, and surely it was moving. Thursey turned onto the narrow path and called to the mare. Her voice sounded strange. What would hear her besides the mare in this eerie place? The white shape seemed to grow smaller.

She hurried faster and the shape moved away from her. It must be the mare. "Oh, wait for me!" Thursey cried. But the mare moved on annoyingly. The water around Thursey was like liquid metal, the moon reflected in it.

The swamp path wound and lost itself among copses of stunted trees, and always just ahead the white shape moved away. Only once did Thursey get a little closer, and then her directions were confused entirely—but surely it was the mare.

Then the shape left the swamp path and plunged into the swamp itself and Thursey, thoroughly frightened, plunged after it, running.

The mud was icy cold, and slimy round her ankles. She called to the mare, and her voice did not seem so lost now because the noise of her splashing accompanied it. The shape ahead took no notice of her. Then by a lonely tree the mare looked back and threw her head in stubborn defiance. Thursey could see her plainly now. She sighed with relief. "Come on, old mare," she cried. "Can't you wait for me?"

The mare flicked her tail and went on.

"Oh please, I need you so," Thursey cried. She was almost in tears.

The mare stopped.

She was knee deep in mud when Thursey got to her and looking very pleased with herself. She drew back her old lips, showed her huge yellow teeth, and nipped Thursey on the arm.

"Oh!" Thursey cried and put the rope on her. "Oh, how horrid you can be!" And then she collapsed against the mare, crying in spite of herself. She told the mare

about the dress and about how cruelly the sisters had acted. She cried and cried against the mare's warm neck, and the mare stood patiently in the mud and did not nip again. Clouds covered the moon so the swamp darkened, and the water grew colder around their feet. But it didn't matter, they were together.

When the mare started back of her own accord toward the swamp path, Thursey was so exhausted she could only follow dumbly, hanging onto the halter. The mare seemed in some haste now to be out of the mud, and soon it was all Thursey could do to trot beside her in the knee-deep muck and to climb up the slick bank toward the swamp path. From slimy water they squelched onto clinging mud—then suddenly ahead of them a second white shape loomed. If the mare had not been beside her, Thursey would surely have followed it. She trembled so her heart seemed to stop and tried to force the mare in another direction, but the stubborn old creature kept on, looking with little interest at the pale shape.

Thursey jerked the halter but it did little good. It's nothing! she thought. It's nothing but a tree. But she wasn't sure.

Then she caught the scent of roses.

"It's roses," she said aloud, wondering. "It's the enchanted rosebush. But it can't be, there's no such thing as enchantment. It's just a plain rosebush. There's no such thing as haunts either," she added sharply and approached the bush straight on.

When she reached it, she was trembling, perhaps with fear, perhaps from anticipation. And overcome with curiosity. How could such a bush grow in these quantities of mud? She stared at the heavily budded branches—the bush was a tall as she was—then leaned against the mare's warm side, thinking. The mare, bored, began to nose among the runners for grass.

An ordinary rosebush. Healthy and rank with growth and crowded with tiny pink blooms. They were clustered, small and perfect, along each supple branch. Thursey took a runner in her hands and not a thorn was there to scratch her. She pulled it free of the bush and held it up in the moonlight. The little roses were scented delicately and finely made as lace.

I might, she thought. Could I? She stared at the roses and felt excitement take her.

Soon she had pulled away an armload of long creepers and laid them across the mare's back. Elated, she gathered more until the pile towered, sweet and heavy. The mare stood head down, nibbling dis-interestedly.

Thursey scrambled up behind her burden, trying not to crush a single rose, and dug in her heels. The mare was tired now and unwilling, but Thursey, stubborn too, kept at her. She dared not think about what she intended to do. She dared not wonder if she *could* do it. She crouched over the scented bundle numb with cold as the mare splashed through the mud toward the road, then started home.

And when they came at last through their own gate, there was Anwin's little donkey standing in the stable yard.

Thursey piled off the mare with her burden almost toppling her and was about to fly into the kitchen to greet Anwin when the little monk stepped out of the shadows by the water trough and took the mare's halter. He eyed the roses but said nothing, though he looked perplexed. Gathering roses in the middle of the night? This night?

"I saw the torn dress," he said at last. "I came back thinking . . ." He looked at the roses again, then at Thursey. Then slowly something began to dawn on him. He began to smile. Then he grinned. Then he laughed out loud. "Well hurry up, child, the night is getting on! I'll see to this old mare."

She flew to the kitchen wondering if Anwin really

had guessed what she was about. She could not even look at the poor torn dress. She dumped the roses on the table, opened the cupboard, and from behind some crocks drew out the hastily sewn cotton model she had made.

She stirred up the fire and put the iron to heat, then drew the kettle from the hob, poured out some luke-warm water, and began to wash the mud and grime from herself, scrubbing until she was pink. Next she ironed the rough cotton model, found her needle and thread, and commenced to put proper stitching into the basted seams.

It seemed hours that Thursey stitched, hurrying as fast as she could, and all the time thinking, I'll never be done. And even if I am, no one can go to the king's ball dressed practically in her nightdress. It's not even bound around the sleeves and neck. Why am I sewing like this in the middle of the night?

But still she sewed faster and could not seem to help herself. All the stubborness in Thursey had risen like a tide, and she would not give in even to good sense.

When Anwin came in to help her, they both sewed as fast as they could, the seams, and then the rose tendrils, twining them around the skirt. Through the open doorway Thursey could see the moon beginning to drop a little, and she could hear the midnight trumpets from the castle, so her heart dropped too—nearly to her toes.

"You don't want to make an entrance while they're at supper, child. Wait until the dancing begins again—these things go on until dawn. There will be no pumpkin to call you back, Thursey, once you are at the palace."

Thursey stared at Anwin. And suddenly all the uncertainty she had fought came flooding out. She lay her needle down and sat looking at her hands. What made her think—*what had ever made her think*—that she could go to the king's ball dressed in common muslin sewn with swamp vines? Everyone would laugh. Her stepsisters would roar; she could almost hear Delilah.

And Gillie—Gillie would be shocked.

"Oh Anwin . . ."

Anwin smiled, patted her hand, sewed his last stitch, and put down his needle. He held the full skirt out wide so the rows and rows of twined roses shone in the candlelight. Then he stood, lifted Thursey to her feet and unbuttoned her old dress so it slid to the floor. He dropped the rose-covered dress over Thursey's head and fastened it. Then he rummaged in the cupboards until he found the silver cord with which Gillie's

100

package had been tied, and, with surprising skill for a man, he began to brush and bind up Thursey's hair.

When at last she looked into the mirror the old monk brought, she could not believe it. Her hair, piled high in a coronet and woven with silver, was a wonder. Her cheeks were pink with excitement. And the dress— oh, the rose-covered dress looked beautiful. She stared, turned, pirouetted. Then she flung her arms around Anwin.

But the old man held her away, and wiped her tears, and said gruffly, "Come, child, the night is getting on." He led her out to the stable yard and handed her up the mounting block just like a real lady, and then he brought the mare.

Oh, the mare had been polished until she shone. Anwin had bathed her, and her hooves were trimmed and blackened. Across her back was a red silk saddle cloth, and atop it shone Augusta's sidesaddle, polished and fine, and the mare was wearing Augusta's riding bridle!

Thursey, torn between shock and hilarity at borrowing Augusta's prized possessions, could only stand grinning at Anwin. The hair in the mare's ears had been trimmed smooth, as had her muzzle and her fetlocks. And her mane was worked carefully with red ribbons into a thick French braid that ran the length of her neck. Her tail was braided the same, and the old creature was arching her neck and thrusting her ears forward comically.

Thursey mounted and seated herself for the first time in a real lady's sidesaddle and took up the reins. "Oh Anwin, do I look a fool?"

"You look . . . like the loveliest princess ever to grace the land. Like a true princess. I told you one day you would know enchantment, and this is the night, Cendrillon. Now off with you. I don't want to see you 'til dawn."

Thursey, never having ridden sidesaddle, felt for an instant as if she were going over backward; but the mare moved with a strange new grace, as if perhaps the old hoyden's pride had been restored, and soon enough they were cantering effortlessly through the moonlight, the mare placing her feet exactly right among the rocks and boulders—though her ears twisted around occasionally with curiosity.

Thursey, her gown spread carefully around her, gave the mare her head gladly and gazed up at the palace. I'm going to the king's ball. I *really* am going. She heard Anwin's voice again, " . . . like the loveliest princess in the land. I told you one day you would know enchantment—like a princess . . ." She lifted the reins and nudged the mare into a faster canter.

But then between village and castle, just at the beginning of the long drive with the lights shining down from all the windows above her and the music so gay, she was suddenly uncertain again. She pulled the mare in and sat still as stone, staring up the hill at the whirl of dancing figures through the windows.

Rows of torches flamed along the walks and drive and among the gardens. A glow of light fell over the arbors and across the sculptured hedges and the balconies; the windows were brilliant. Torchlight shone on the coachmen who were rubbing down the waiting carriage horses. The mare took a few tentative steps as Thursey sat staring, and Thursey could see the footmen at the top of the marble stairs that led up to the ballroom. She could see a bit of the chandelier inside, and the dancers; the mare pulled suddenly at the bit and began to walk up the drive. The grooms stopped their work and watched. A strange old mare, a strangely clad girl riding up to the palace alone on a night meant for escorts and carriages and laughing parties. A lone girl with swamp roses sewn on her dress. In a panic Thursey pulled the mare round.

I can't. Oh I can't. Not in muslin and swamp roses!

They'll all be wearing satin and velvet and Belgium lace and ermine—I can't go up there. Whatever made me think I could? She leaned over the mare and dug her heels in hard.

But the old mare, mesmerized by the light and glitter and the music, swung stubbornly to face the palace. And somewhere inside Thursey, then, a similar stubbornness burst forth, and made her want to go on.

What had she sewn half the night for if she was going to run away? What would Anwin say if she came home? She grasped at her shredded courage, gave the mare her head, and rode straight for the marble stairs.

A footman took the mare's bridle and did not laugh, and another handed Thursey down as carefully as any lady.

Thursey gazed above her, up the stairs.

The marble flight rose like a mountain. At the very top, the liveried footmen stared straight ahead of them. And though the music was bright, a hush held the night suspended—a hush within herself, as if her own heart had ceased to beat. If she had come early in a group, with her sisters—she quailed, almost turned, then with determination she lifted the hem of her skirt as a real lady would and began to ascend the stairs. Her heart pounded but she made herself go on; her feet seemed very heavy, even in Anwin's silver slippers. She stared down at them and tried to think of Anwin's kindness as she mounted one step, then the next.

Could I really have looked the way I thought in the mirror? Could I have looked beautiful, as Anwin said? Or was it only what I wanted to see? The music swept around her and she could hear laughter and happy voices. One step, another. *Do* I look all right? Will everyone laugh at me? Her skirts rustled reassuringly, and billowed out around her with the stiffness the roses gave them. Halfway to the top she paused, and glanced upward at the landing.

The footmen still stared straight ahead, as immobile as the marble columns that supported the overhanging roof. But now there was another figure standing above her just at the head of the stairs. A tall young man dressed in dark velvet and gathered linen and white gloves. He was looking down at her, not quite smiling. He was waiting for her, his hand held out to her. She couldn't believe what she saw. She stood staring and forgot her own uncertainties as she looked and looked. Gillie! It was Gillie!

How elegant he was. How *could* he be dressed like that? How could he be here on the ballroom steps? She felt giddy inside herself, as if the steps were rocking. Gillie had never told her *he'd* be at the ball.

But of course the king had said all the people; he must have meant the servants, too. Though Gillie didn't look like any servant, not dressed like that. Nor like a goatherd either. He looked quite wonderful; and his blue eyes were steady on hers. She took one tentative step and tried to speak, but only a small croak came out. Was he laughing underneath that serious look? He held his finger to his lips, and she thought, He's playing a game! That's it. The liverymen have dressed Gillie up for the ball.

But these weren't livery clothes. These were far richer, far finer. She climbed the stairs toward him, her heart pounding. Gillie did not move, but his eyes urged her on: she felt as if her whole life depended on this moment.

When she reached the top at last, Gillie took her hand and drew her to him so she went giddy indeed; she was in his arms, was being swept through the great doors close to Gillie, was on the polished ballroom floor, whirling, lifted by the music, close to Gillie. . . .

The light from a thousand candles set in crystal chandeliers shimmered over them, catching the flash of instruments where the orchestra played on a raised gallery; the colors of the dancers flashed and changed as Gillie whirled her—she hadn't known she could dance like this, like flying . . . surely she was dreaming, but she didn't care, she willed herself never to wake. She could feel the music in her blood like something alive, could feel the brush of other dancers as they circled, could feel her skirt whirl and dip, and smell the faint scent of crushed roses where she was pressed tight against Gillie—if this was a dream, this enchantment, she would not let it end. But Gillie, so close, Gillie was too real for any dream. The faces around them were happy, smiling, were watching them sometimes. She felt as elegant as any woman there, and she felt cherished and loved—and then suddenly she saw Augusta scowling from the sidelines, her dress dark against the brightness, her venom directed at Thursey, and she felt a stab of fear.

But what could Augusta do? Not run onto the dance floor and jerk her away! The vision of that, the dark square figure running among the dancers, was so funny that Thursey buried her face against Gillie's shoulder in a sudden fit of mirth.

Oh, if this was a dream, this heady nearness to Gillie, she *would not* let it end.

But then Druscilla whirled close, dancing with the

fishmonger—a comical sight—and Thursey wondered what the stepsisters would do to her after the ball when she was home again. "Oh Gillie," she blurted, suddenly coming to earth.

"Shhh. They can't touch you."

Not now, she thought. After the ball they will. Oh well, maybe there isn't any later, maybe I'll never wake up. I won't think about it. Gillie swung her in front of one of the long ballroom mirrors, and the reflection of the two of them spun and paused; she could hardly believe it was herself and Gillie she saw. Surely Gillie was the handsomest man in the ballroom. And her own reflection—oh, yes, her own reflection pleased her now, for she looked as if she belonged in Gillie's arms . . . his lips brushed her hair as he bent to whisper. . . .

Later, at a pause in the music, he held her away. "You look beautiful; it's the most sensational dress in the ballroom, all the women are staring with envy. But? . . ."

Thursey looked at him with chagrin. "She tore it into pieces," she whispered miserably. "Your beautiful dress, Gillie." She felt again the pain of that moment. "At the very last minute they found it, and Augusta—into pieces and pieces—"

"*Shh* . . . it's all right, it's all right. You did handsomely in spite of it," he said admiringly. The music lifted into a strong waltz, and they were carried on it as on a tide so her feet hardly touched the floor. "But where did you find the roses? I don't remember roses in the village, not like these."

"The swamp roses, Gillie. It was the mare found them. She—if she hadn't run off—it was almost as if she meant me to see them."

"Are you saying? . . ."

"I don't know what I'm saying. Yes," she cried, a gay silliness taking her. Drunk with the music and the dancing, drunk with his closeness, she laughed up at him. "It was just as in the stories, a kind of magic just like . . ." and then she stared at him, confounded.

"Just like what?"

"But in the stories . . ."

"In the stories . . . *what?*"

"In the stories . . ."

"In the stories there's a prince," Gillie answered quietly. He held her away then. "So the story has come true."

She stared at him and stumbled and wanted to stop dancing. She felt dazed, then frightened. She had known it from the moment she looked up and saw him at the head of the stairs, but she had not admitted it.

109

She had not really known she knew. Gillie. Gillie, with whom she had sat among the hills. Gillie . . . and she saw the truth of it coldly and clearly: Gillie was not the same now, was not the Gillie she knew. That Gillie was lost to her forever. Nothing could be the same now. They would not walk on the hills again and take their lunch from a basket. They were different now, she and Gillie.

But Gillie was grinning without a care, teasing. "Do you know you've shown yourself to a prince in your nightdress? And ridden with your skirts hiked up in front of him like any hoyden girl?"

She tried to smile but she could not. You can love a goatherd and feel there is some hope. But to love a prince. . . .

He would dance with her this one night, and then— and then—she saw he was still smiling, but her own heart was like lead. "Oh Gillie, not the prince," she said in spite of herself. She could not help the tear that came.

He stared at her, puzzled. Then he swept her from the ballroom and out a side door onto the terrace. There they stood facing each other silently in the shadow of a portico.

She wiped the tear and fought the further tears that

threatened. She hadn't meant to cry. Oh, how could she spoil this beautiful evening. She bit her lip and made herself smile. "I'm sorry, Gillie—it's just—it's the surprise of it, I guess." She didn't know how to tell him what she felt. She could not.

"Thursey, I—Thursey . . ." He seemed almost shy suddenly, not like the Gillie she knew. He was feeling sorry for her, that was it. He was trying to think how to tell her he would never see her again. "Thursey, I want . . ." But they were interrupted.

". . . here—find them here." Oh, it was Augusta!

". . . had her nerve, and where did she get *that* dress, I thought . . ."

"There! There they are, in the shadows!"

Thursey turned, the last joy of the night stifled, and watched the three storm across the terrace, Augusta in full steam and the other two directly in her wake. Druscilla was squinting, the better to see Thursey's features; and Delilah was leaning forward as if the added few inches would help her make out what it was she was not sure about.

Thursey, resigned, stepped out of the shadows to face them.

But Gillie was quicker. He stood between Thursey and Augusta, as the stepmother reached for her.

111

Augusta scowled at him. "Get out of my way! We thought you were the prince, you charlatan. Then we saw you were not. You've *deceived* them, you've deceived everyone at the ball! Where is the real prince? And let me have *her*, she's my charge!" She reached for Thursey again. "*She* belongs in the kitchen, and *you*—you belong in the stable yard with your goats!"

Thursey's face flamed. She must get them out of here, get them away at once.

"It's just like I said," Druscilla cried loudly, reaching rudely to feel the cloth of Gillie's sleeve, the while staring at him as if he were a servant. "It's like I said, they've dressed the goatherd up because he looks healthy, they thought to make out the prince was healed and—"

"*I* think . . ." Delilah interrupted.

But Gillie looked at them so coldly, all three were silenced. His expression was truly fierce. Then a twitch of laughter twisted the corner of his mouth; he tried to hide it, but he could not. He doubled over suddenly with laughter, roaring.

The stepsisters and Augusta stared. After a long moment, when Gillie kept laughing, they began to shout at him. "Stop it!" Druscilla screamed, "*You* can't . . ."

"We won't tolerate . . ."

"Cease at once . . ."

Gillie roared the louder, and Thursey, infected, nearly choked with laughter. Never in her life had she laughed in her stepmother's face. Now she could not stop. She hid her face and shook with laughter, nearly crying with it.

She looked up to see a page standing before Gillie, glancing with surprise at the three shouting women. "Your highness . . ." the page began.

"*Don't* call him 'your highness,'" Augusta shouted. "Don't you know an imposter when you see one!"

The boy's gaze showed amazement at Augusta's behavior; then he returned his attention to Gillie. "Your highness . . ." His voice was more emphatic now. "The king bids . . ."

Augusta stepped forward. "You, boy, stop that muttering and call the king at once. Call the guard! This is an imposter; he's not the prince at all! Can't you see! You must be an imbecile not to know your own prince!" Her face had grown beet red.

The page looked at her, now, as if she were quite mad. Then, deliberately, he turned his back on her. "Your highness," he said patiently, "the king bids you bring your partner to be presented to him and the queen. And he spoke of the sword . . ."

Now Augusta flew into such a rage that both the page and Gillie drew back, and Thursey stared in dismay. "You can't know this—this dung-pusher for the prince! You're lying, ignorant clod!"

But the young page's patience was exhausted. "I know him!" he cried hotly, turning his full attention on Augusta. "I have known Edward Gillian, Prince of Gies, all my life, madam! I served him faithfully at Carthemas these two years past and hope to serve him 'til I die!"

Gillie was grinning at the boy's indignant anger. He put a hand on the page's shoulder and looked coldly at Augusta. "Do you call my page a liar, old woman? And who are you to speak of this lady as your charge? My page is no liar, just as Thursey is not your charge. Not in any way. She is your landlord, for it is her inn you occupy. And it is to her you will answer for its keeping. She is beholden to no one, unless it would be the people of Gies in the same manner as I am—for she may be their princess soon. If she is willing," he added gently.

Thursey stared at him, confounded. What was he saying? "You didn't tell me, Gillie. You didn't tell me. . . ." Did he mean he loved her?

"Didn't tell you I was the prince? But it would have

made a strangeness between us. I wanted you to love me as I was, as a goatherd, not as the Prince of Gies." And then he added softly, "Could you, Thursey? Could you love me as I am now?"

"Yes. Oh, yes, Gillie, I could!"

WHEN Thursey had mopped her tears, Gillie took her hand, gave the stepsisters and Augusta a last, amused look, and spoke quietly to the page. "Tell my father we will come now. Take the Sword of Balskak from its resting place and lay it by the king's hand."

He led Thursey to the gallery, where she knelt before the seated king and queen. She dared not gaze up at them. But Gillie raised her chin and made her look, and she saw the king was smiling. Across his knees lay a sword, old and battered. The music in the ballroom was silenced as Gillie turned to face the stilled dancers. He drew them forward with a look, with a gesture. He was not a goatherd now, there was no question who he was. Thursey felt she hardly knew him as he stood speaking to the assembled citizens of Gies so softly, but with such authority.

AFTERWARD she felt so faint she thought she could not walk from the ballroom. And when they sat alone in the garden she was shaken still. Gillie brought her wine and some supper, but she sat staring at the plate knowing she couldn't eat.

"Drink," Gillie said. "Eat a little, Thursey. When did you eat last?"

"I don't know." She sipped the wine and found it helped. "You knew all along, Gillie! You knew it was my father who . . . that it was he who wielded the Sword of Balkskak." There in the ballroom, as she had stood facing Gillie, she had been swept with a sadness and longing for her father and with a joy for him, that she could hardly deal with. There were no tears, but her eyes were as heavy and full as her heart as Gillie placed the sword in her outstretched hands.

"I didn't know until you told me your father had been hurt in the mill. Even then, not at first. I was nearly unconscious during the battle. I was so weak I couldn't lift my head, let alone my hand to help him. It was only when you mentioned the two missing fingers that the picture came back to me, of a tall blond man fighting practically on top of me with his maimed right hand flung back so he wielded the sword with his left. A maimed hand with two fingers missing.

"My father has always vowed that the wielder of the sword would be presented it in ceremony in the

great hall. You are his only kin, Thursey. Don't tell me you didn't enjoy the spectacle your stepmother made, trying to claim the sword in your stead." He started to grin, then pulled his face into a serious expression. "You mean you didn't like seeing the king put her down?"

She bent over, shaken with sudden mirth. "Yes. Oh, yes, Gillie, you . . ." But then she straightened up and stared at him. "But you haven't told me everything. Why did you pose as a goatherd? Why did you come back to your own country disguised? And who was looking out of the carriage next to the queen? What—"

He hushed her, then grinned again. "Did you never guess who I was?"

"No. Nor did anyone else. How could I? I thought you were very handsome. I thought Carthemas must be a special place to have a goatherd like you, but . . ."

"Carthemas is a wonderful place. Listen, Thursey, even when I was small I wasn't allowed my freedom among the hills and pastures of Gies. I was always in the gardens of the palace, then later with a dozen or more of the king's company or in a hunting party. And at the summer palace it was the same, I was never on my own. Then we were attacked and I was wounded right off, and there was the long journey, bound in a wagon with my mother, as we were taken to Balkskak. And then the time of sickness and my leg paining me, and my mother so ill—always confinement. I never knew what it was to be on my own. The prison cell was the first time I was ever really alone, and then there were walls around me. When we were rescued and taken to Carthemas—I think my father believed we would both die, it was a desperate thing he did to journey all the way with us secretly, in the night— when we were taken there and I began to mend and to be allowed to roam freely over the island, it was an amazement to me. I was alone for the first time on the hills in the wind, and you can't imagine the freedom I felt. I think that, as much as the goat milk, helped to cure me. When it was time to return, I didn't want this old life again so soon. I told my father I would not return at all unless I had it my way. And my way was to become the goatherd, and get to know Gies and this village in a way I never could have otherwise."

"But who was in the carriage?"

"A page with powdered face. The few trusted servants and members of the court who knew were pledged to secrecy. I had not been known well in the village, and I was less than twelve when I left it the last time. You can't imagine the thrill of walking into the village that day as if I were no one and having no attention paid to me, just to see it as it is seen by everyone else— and hear them shout for the prince, I could hardly keep from laughing at that."

THEY were married on a fair summer day, when the sky was washed with blue and the rock-strewn hills ablaze with the brilliant green of new grass. They were not married by the bishop as was the custom, but by Anwin in his plain brown habit, which contrasted mightily with the pomp of the proceedings, with the fine regalia of the king and his queen and the court.

And Anwin said, "It turned out just as an enchantment should."

"But Anwin, it wasn't an enchantment really, it just—"

"Yes, child, it was the greatest enchantment of all." He winked at the prince. "Gillie understood all along what the enchantment was."

And though there were wedding gifts that dazzled Thursey's eyes, the gift that made her cry was from Anwin. It was a carved hazelwood chest just large enough to hold her painted books, and all the books were there inside, safe and bright.

On the lid of the chest Anwin had carved three words:

ENCHANTMENT IS FOREVER.

When they rode away on their honeymoon, the bride was finely mounted on a liveried, silver-shod, beautifully groomed white mare who glared rheumily at the prince's fiery stallion and showed her big teeth at him in a fierce and friendly gesture of comaraderie.

The princess rode her proudly, and she would have no other.

"Are you happy?" asked the prince.

"Oh, I am happy, Gillie."

And he kissed her as they rode away down the high road, where pilgrims traveled, and gleemen, where the king's lords journeyed amidst minstrels and knights and herbalists and gypsy caravans to all the reaches of Gies and beyond, to Bruges and Apulia and Calabria and to countries so small one had never heard of them.

The End

Made in the USA
San Bernardino, CA
20 July 2016